NORTHERN
FUTURES

Praise for Mark Anthony Ayling

'Mark Ayling has a delightful story sense and tells those stories in remarkable ways. We've published him frequently in "Perihelion." He always brings a fabulous sense of wonder to the pages of our webzine. He is constantly a reader favorite, and I personally enjoy his stories immeasurably. Can't wait to read his next manuscript.'
    ~Sam Bellotto Jr., Editor, Perihelion Online Science Fiction Magazine

'I've been involved in the creative writing racket since 1956. About 10 years ago I started producing an anthology series, Twisted Tails. When I put out a call for submissions for the most recent volume, *Twisted Tails IX: Wunderkind*, I received a manuscript from Mark Ayling. I am a tough editor and the acceptance rate for these anthologies has averaged around 12%.

Mr. Ayling made it in that 12%. He has a fresh voice that had me engaged within three lines. His imaginative, intense approach gained immediate acceptance, and his story, "Prodigious," became part of the Wunderkind project. Mark Ayling's work makes a delightful read, especially if the reader has a somewhat warped sense of humor and likes the unusual.'
    ~J. Richard Jacobs, Editor, Twisted Tails

NORTHERN FUTURES

MARK ANTHONY AYLING

LILLICAT PUBLISHERS
USA

Northern Futures

Lillicat Publishers books may be ordered through booksellers or by contacting Lillicat Publishers at www.lillicatpublishers.com.

POD ISBN: 978-1-945646-07-2
EPUB ISBN: 978-1-945646-08-9
MOBI ISBN: 978-1-945646-09-6

Northern Futures is dedicated to my wife and two children, without whom, none of this would be possible.

Contents

ACKNOWLEDGEMENTS

Thanks in no particular order to:

Mum and Dad, cause you're great; to Elaine, my wife, for tolerating me for over a decade; Anne, my mother in law, for also tolerating me for over a decade; to Sam and Molly for being beautiful; to my sister Tracey and her husband Ste, to my nieces Emma and Kelly for putting up with my ranting, to the Gillespie mob, which is comprised of my good friend Ste, his wife Trace, and their daughters Holly, Kasey and Boo for Italy and France and everything in between, to Alan and Jennie and clan for all the food and kindness, the late night gaming sessions and camping trips, to Chris OB and Claire for the music and dancing; to all my colleagues toiling endlessly to maintain and improve mental healthcare provision and quality in the NHS both past and present, you all deserve more thanks than I'm able to provide in three paltry lines; to all my students who have had to put up with my music and driving over the years; to Dave Straughan, Ed O'Hara (no relation to Prescott), Matt Brazil, Simon Birch-Machin, and everyone else from Chester, you know who you are; to everyone on my social media, hi and thanks; to all the fans at Salford Red Devils Rugby League, for your stoicism; to St. Helens for being my home town and Salford for adopting me; to anyone I've missed, and finally to anyone who ever read, commented on, moaned about, or simply didn't finish one of my stories in the last thirty or so years.
Thanks for everything.
I hope you enjoy reading the stories in here.

Special mention to:
Sam Bellotto Jr. at Perihelion Online Science Fiction Magazine, for originally editing and publishing some of the

stories in this collection, whose support and advice over the last few years has been priceless.

Also, thanks to J. Richard Jacobs for *Twisted Tails* and the opportunity to finally get a horror story in print.

Thanks to Carrol Fix and everyone at Lillicat Publishers for the opportunity, support, and advice.

Thanks to the Manchester Speculative Fiction Group who are brightening weekdays up for me twice a month with stories and banter.

Thanks to everyone involved in the creative writing course at the Recovery Academy at Prestwich Hospital, my involvement so far has been a pleasure.

Finally, I would like to say Hello to Jason Isaacs . . . mostly because I can.

Silas Marvel Investigates is dedicated to Claire and Chris, as Silas would more than likely have had rubbish taste in music without them.

Vegan State is for all my food loving buddies everywhere, vegan, vegetarian and carnivore alike.

Bodies, meanwhile, owes a debt of gratitude to my old friend, Ed, for obvious reasons.

When the desperate widow of a recently murdered Clocker attends the offices of Silas Marvel Investigations to retain his services, Marvel accepts the case. However, what should be a relatively straightforward investigation is much more complicated than it first appears.

SILAS MARVEL INVESTIGATES

Silas Marvel, balding, middle aged, though still relatively healthy in spite of his lack of enhancements, detective, Luddite, vinyl lover, and disco fanatic, stumbled into his office from the adjoining bathroom. Up until a moment ago, he'd been sat on the toilet. He was listening to Gloria Gaynor while noisily voiding his bowels. An image had appeared, disturbing his ablutions, projected from a drone fixed to the wall above the sink. The image was fuzzy since the drone was on the fritz. He could just make out a client, recently entered into his office space, fiddling with the Anglepoise on the desk, twisting the head about, seemingly perplexed by its functionality. The Anglepoise, which was an original 1227 design from the first half of the twentieth century with fully functioning spring technology and custom safety-switch to facilitate luminosity, routinely baffled clients. The number of people he'd caught messing with it, twisting the lamp head about and talking to it like it was an AI, always managed to bring a smile to his face.

Silas flushed the toilet. He waved the image away. He clambered off the loo, which thanked him for his deposit. He careened off a filing cabinet on entrance, cursed, greeted his client with a wave of his hand, and negotiated a position behind his overcrowded desk.

'Good afternoon,' he said. 'How can I be of assistance?'

Seated on an oxblood leather upholstered club chair from the 1930's and set against the backdrop of Marvel's vintage boutique, with its antique cameras, hand crafted pottery items, ancient discarded paper books, wall fans, and dusty record crates, the client reclined incongruously.

Her name was Jane Waterman and she was recently a widow.

Marvel inventoried. She was probably around forty, slim, neat looking, a one-time beauty, now established and sensual. She was sheathed in black. She wore black gloves up to her elbows and black knee boots with red lace-ups. There was some kind of mourning tattoo burned on her face. It was a holo-burn and would fade once the mourning period was completed.

Her hair, a digitally enhanced, fake, lustrous, tech pile, which bobbed as she spoke and was unable to fix its colour, focused Marvel's attention. He tried to avoid staring but it was difficult not to gawp at it.

'Your hair's glitching,' he noted.

'It does that when I feel upset.'

The widow snuffled, removed an inhaler from her brassiere, placed it between her lips, and inhaled deeply. She was immediately more relaxed. It was probably a sedative of some kind. Research showed that in recent years there was an increase in the use of non-prescription pharmaceuticals to manage stress. The woman's hair subsequently settled. Blood suffused her cheeks. Her posture melted further, rendering her looser and more open.

'My husband has been murdered,' she said amicably. 'I need someone to find the killer. I've come here to hire you. I would like you to apprehend them.'

ORAL LOG OF SILAS MARVEL, RE: THE KILLING OF BRIAN WATERMAN IN MARCH OF THIS YEAR: STREAMING COMMENCE.

To start with then, we have a wife, in mourning for her recently-dead husband, something of a looker though her hair could do with a tune up. Then there's the husband,

2

Brian Waterman, less pretty, killed in a hijacking incident working a route through the lower city. Ex services, fifty years old, a problem drinker arrested twice for brawling, ten years as a Clocker following discharge from the army, married fifteen years to Jane, no children, one further conviction for domestic violence, though the charges were dropped by the wife following arrest.

What else do we know? Brian Waterman, a professional Clocker, was fully qualified in the use of Reset. Courier firms, such as Getters Incorporated, use Reset technology to defend against attack. Initially developed by the Anaphylaxis Corporation to support soldiers in frontline combat scenarios, the technology is used today in the protection of couriers. You have to hold a license to use it. Time wastage being illegal, it's heavily regulated.

Couriers registered with a licensed company are trained in the use of Reset. Couriers who have been trained in Reset are known as Clockers or Cyclers.

Brian Waterman, the longest serving Clocker on Getter's payroll, was well regarded at the firm. His colleagues referred to him as Safe Hands. He always delivered his packages on time. His completion rate was 100%.

Clockers have the ability to reset time. At any point, along a pre-arranged postal route, a Clocker, or Cycler, depending on your preference, can activate their stop-clock. The clock, a neurological implant bedded into the cerebellum, enables Clockers to reverse their continuum. It only works over relatively short spans. Up to one hour is fine; any more than that, there's a permanent risk of brain damage.

In order to reset, the Clocker utters a password, which only they have access to. Their vocal signature triggers the mechanism and they are immediately recycled to their prearranged coordinates. Each reset is unique, thus rendering the technology tamperproof in the field.

We have a timeline of sorts. The Clocker commences his route for the courier company Getters, gets all the way to the end and has to trigger his clock for an unknown reason. Then, as soon as he cycles back, he is murdered on arrival.

The nature of the murder signposts the Burberry twins, gangsters from the lower city, whose trademark sign-off is brutal and inimitable . . .

There's no concrete evidence of their involvement in the crime, but the way it was arranged is definitely their MO. The way the victim was killed, the hands and feet bound with wire, the victim blindfolded with a rag soaked in bleach, two bullets to the head, both kidneys removed via posthumous surgery, it all indicates a Burberry execution. Must have been the work of an AI too, a killer on the twin's payroll, the precision and speed of the killing would have been impossible for a human to achieve. Still . . . something doesn't tally. There's something off with the scene. I can't pin it down. I checked the crime scene stills provided by the firm. Projected them in the office. Worked my way around them with help from my AI system. However, no matter how many close-ups of major surgery I analyze, I cannot identify what's causing my suspicions.
STOP.

Duty sergeant Ed Gatsby, who worked the homicide desk at the GMP, was a willing collaborator in Marvel's investigations. Marvel had retrieved Gatsby's daughter, holed up in a London squat, strung out on illegal Memware products, after the sergeant solicited him to investigate her disappearance. He'd pulled the case file at Marvel's request, made a copy, and sent it to him via a postal drone with its ID filed off.

The police had reached similar conclusions to Marvel. Despite the crime scene indicating the Burberry Twins' involvement, there was nothing irrefutable to tie them to the killing. The police investigation had stalled. Their enthusiasm had flamed out. The trail had gone cold. There were no more leads to be followed up. It helped that the company involved wanted to minimize publicity. The case was being shelved and other concerns taking precedence.

EXTRACT FROM INITIAL INTERVIEW WITH MRS.
WATERMAN REGARDING THE MURDER OF HER
HUSBAND IN MARCH OF THIS YEAR:

STREAMING COMMENCE.

SILAS MARVEL: If you could just state for the record your name and relationship to the deceased, when you're ready, we can begin with the interview.

MRS WATERMAN: Okay. Well. My name is Jane Francis Waterman. I was the wife of the deceased while he was alive. I'm his widow now, since he was recently murdered.

SILAS MARVEL: Okay, you said in your original statement, Mrs. Waterman, the night of your husband's murder, that you were, and I quote, "attending a charity event in the city." Is this correct?

MRS WATERMAN: It is correct, yes. I work for a charity called Retek. Basically the charity provides support for homeless AI's and clones. The event was organized to develop awareness of the situation. A number of celebrities and officials attended, local media representatives and rights campaigners.

SILAS MARVEL: I take it your attendance at this event can be verified?

MRS WATERMAN: A couple of hundred people could verify my attendance.

PAUSE.

SILAS MARVEL: For the record, Mrs. Waterman, could you state when it was that you last saw your husband?

MRS WATERMAN: An hour before his shift started. He was withdrawing from alcohol at the time, wasn't feeling very well, getting the shakes, that sort of thing. He was thinking of calling in sick. I convinced him to go to work. He took his medication and seemed to be feeling better . . .

SILAS MARVEL: Was there anything different about him? Did he say anything or behave differently to usual? Was he nervous or frightened perhaps? Did he mention anything that may have caused you concern?

MRS WATERMAN: No. I'm afraid he didn't, or not that I noticed at any rate. There's the possibility I was distracted due the event I was attending. I wish I had noticed something. I could have prevented him from working . . .

SILAS MARVEL: *Finally, Mrs. Waterman, I'd just like to ask, could you describe your relationship with your husband for me? Was it a good relationship? Was it a difficult relationship?*

MRS WATERMAN: *The relationship was difficult. The love was gone from the marriage. He had his work. He had his AI prostitutes to keep him busy. He drank a lot. He was occasionally violent. We were the happy couple publicly, social engagements, that sort of thing, however privately we were struggling . . . Incidentally, before you ask, and I dare say you will ask, we might as well address it, I have benefitted from my husband's passing. I won't deny the life insurance paid well. Also, I'm to receive a settlement from Getters that was a part of the contract if my husband came to harm. Still. I may have stood to benefit from his death, but that doesn't mean I'm responsible for his murder. The fact remains that I loved him once and I want his killer brought to justice to pay for their crimes.*

SILAS MARVEL: *Okay, that's all the questions I had for you at this time . . . Interview terminated at 16:30, on the date logged.*

MRS WATERMAN: *Please don't hesitate to contact me if you require any further information detective.*
STOP.

ORAL LOG OF SILAS MARVEL, RE: THE KILLING OF BRIAN WATERMAN IN MARCH OF THIS YEAR: STREAMING RESUME.

Fact is the evidence points to the twin's. Speaking hypothetically, it's probable the twins rigged the hijack, likely with the help of an insider at Getters, planted someone at the end of the route to influence the reset. Then, once the reset was completed an AI on the twins payroll with surgeon's hands and a yen for human vivisection, executed the Clocker, removed the package then completed their getaway before anyone was aware.

Still if that happened, (and the evidence all but screams it did,) why would the twins, unimaginative extortionists more inclined to protection rackets and online gambling than mail robberies fraught with peril, bother to jack an experienced Clocker? It isn't their usual line of work, what did they have to gain from engaging in such a venture?

Perhaps they're diversifying. Maybe they're expanding their operation? It isn't so unfeasible. All alternative suppositions are limited.
STOP.

The police managed to do one useful thing before dumping the case. They checked out the origins of the package and who the recipient was meant to be. The return address was a fabrication. The name of the sender was also false. The same applied to the recipient. According to the file, when police checked the address, it turned out to be a derelict overrun with Memware addicts.

Marvel began to wonder . . . was the Clocker the target and the package a smokescreen? Was the package the target and the Clocker collateral damage? One thing was certain. This wasn't a straightforward hijack. The more he considered it, the more complex the case appeared.

ORAL LOG OF SILAS MARVEL, RE: THE KILLING OF BRIAN WATERMAN IN MARCH OF THIS YEAR: STREAMING RESUME.

Waterman completed his route. This much is established. Something freaked him at his destination. This is also reasonable to assume. He triggered the clock mechanism, was cycled back fifteen minutes and it was at this point he was attacked and brutally terminated.

When Getters checked the clock, to see how many jumps he did no other jumps were indicated. There was no overtime accrued. Just a single jump to the spot he was killed at.

The killer was an AI of that there is little doubt. As to who the person or persons were at the end of the route, this is proving more difficult to establish. Was it the recipient? Was it a third party perhaps? Or maybe the Clocker was in on it? Perhaps there wasn't a third party. He may have lied about the danger before initiating his cycle. Maybe he was meeting his killer. Maybe he knew about the hijack.

Perhaps he was double crossed and killed to maintain his silence.

The only people privy to information pertaining to the route are the router and the Clocker. This means the Clocker might have been in on it from the start. Alternatively, maybe the router was an accessory? Given that Reset is foolproof and murder shouldn't be possible, not without the involvement of the Clocker or the router, how could one of them not have been involved?

The router, in collaboration with the AI system he's linked with, finalizes the route three days in advance. This allows time to formulate contingency plans. This is in the unlikely event of an incident occurring.

The Clocker is informed at the commencement of their shift. The less they know—more importantly, the later they know it—the less likelihood there is of them sabotaging the delivery.

This means the Clocker didn't relay information to a third party. There wasn't enough time to send that information safely. He would've been detected after it was sent. He would have been apprehended before the run finished. Someone else, the router, or someone with access to the router must have been—oh fuck, shit, fucking coffee fucking bastard—

STOP.

STREAMING RESUME.

With the Clocker no longer a suspect, or not a prime suspect at any rate, the router seems the logical culprit in this. However, the router seems too obvious. The router would've known people would get suspicious, unless he's unutterably stupid, and since it's not the sort of job a moron could do, a relentlessly stupid router is highly unlikely. There had to be an inside man, someone close to the router, with access to the AI and by extension the Clocker.

STOP.

Marvel arranged an interview with the router, Harry Wellens, an overweight former biological. Harry was thirty something, married, loaded with enhancements, hardware of every kind, exotic plug-ins, neurological implants, the works.

The interview was difficult. Harry was distracted throughout. He denied any knowledge of the hijack/murder and spent most of its duration fondling an appendage.

Marvel tired of the blubbery hybrid. He was whining about his work and how he needed to be plugged in. Marvel opted to abandon the interview. But before throwing the towel in, in a last ditch attempt at salvaging the meeting, he interrogated Wellens using standardized C + B., "Cock and Bull", as it was known, was a quick-fire lie-detector test for officers in the field, using a series of closed questions. Marvel had adopted the technique for professional reasons. It wouldn't hold up in a court of law, but it was a useful tool to deploy when trying to establish the truthfulness of witnesses and suspects at short notice.

Marvel completed the test with an aggressive Q + A focused around the router's potential culpability. He asked him the questions, repeating and intensifying them with each go round, and mixing slightly to provoke a response.

EXTRACT FROM COCK AND BULL INTERVIEW
WITH HARRY WELLENS REGARDING THE MURDER
OF BRIAN WATERMAN IN MARCH OF THIS YEAR.
STREAMING COMMENCE.

Silas Marvel: *Did you kill the clocker?*
Harry Wellens: *No.*
Silas Marvel: *Did you know the person responsible for his death?*
Harry Wellens: *No*
Silas Marvel: *Were you involved in the plot to kill "Safe Hands"?*
Harry Wellens: *No.*
Silas Marvel: *Did you knowingly provide route details to the clocker's killer?*
Harry Wellens: *NO!*
STOP.

This went on for some time. However, the more intense the questioning became the more Wellens' increasingly irritable one word rejoinders confirmed his innocence. Wellens breezed the C +B assessment, victory pennants trailing in his wake. He knew nothing about the murder. The interview was a complete washout.

Marvel returned to his office, wending his way dejectedly through the city, back across the River Irwell into Salford, along the historical length of Chapel St, past the old cinema and the former New Oxford public house, pausing for take-out coffee and homemade Eccles cakes at Molly's Deli, before arriving damply at his office, the crumbling brick façade of a former Victorian chartered accountants. The building was hunched today, bowed under the weight of its ageing slate roof. An engraved brass plaque on the door blandly denoted his name and occupation. You had to get close up to be certain what was inscribed on it.

Marvel locked the door. He devoured the Eccles cake and industrial strength coffee. He played Grace Jones on an antique CD system jacked into a temperamental AI, the controls for which were located above the cistern in the bathroom. He projected the police report Gatsby had provided round his office and began to pick through it again to ascertain whether there was anything he'd missed worth investigating further.

According to the report, police investigation of the trigger point had been limited. Most of the mediocre work done focused on the actual crime scene. Meanwhile, the point the Clocker cycled at was given less consideration. There was also the fact that the crime scene still rankled Marvel. There was something staged about it that didn't sit well with him. Perhaps, if he started at the end, where the Clocker cycled, he might find something the police had overlooked. At the very least it would be a trip out. He could maybe stop for lunch on the way and charge the expenses to his account with the widow.

He contacted the widow to update her with his findings, having promised to check in every day about his progress. Once the call ended, he considered his next move. The idea of inspecting the end of the route to ascertain if the police overlooked anything seemed logical. With that in mind, he decided on a field trip. He was feeling desperate. He'd found in the past that this was often when something revealed itself, some previously unknown variable that joined the dots to reveal a bigger picture.

Time to call in the tactical support. Marvel left a message for Hollyz5218, dialed straight into her neurological link. She was probably charging up in sleep mode or surfing online and unable to pick up the call, which wasn't a problem necessarily, since she usually called back once she'd downloaded the message.

Hollyz5218, ex police forensics model, had been honorably discharged from the service these ten years, working the private sector consulting for insurance firms and corporations. Every so often, she put the hours in for Marvel, being, as she was, in thrall to the old world exploratory charms of Marvel Investigations Inc.

Marvel harbored a lot of affection for Holly, an AI with the strength to carve a life out for herself in the biological world, after years of indentured servitude. Some of his admiration was reserved for her impressive ocular abilities. Essentially, Holly was able to zoom and magnify in real time and record detailed images for internal playback. She had an astonishing synthetic brain that enabled her to analyze and process a crime scene in the time that it took for Marvel's coffee to cool down.

She also occasionally acted as Marvel's social escort, whenever he needed a chaperone, a favor Marvel reciprocated whenever it was required of him. He would deflect creepy biologicals who would hit on her, thinking she was turning tricks, while she made him look sophisticated, or less disheveled at any rate. This was no mean feat, as anyone who had met Marvel was able to affirm. He had a way of making even the most refined environments sloppier. His prolonged presence would lower the tone to such an extent people often became shabbier by osmosis.

'Hi, Holly, it's Marvel here. I've a favor to ask. I need your eyes for a case I'm working on, a day's work I reckon, lower city, complex homicide investigation. You'll probably need a weapon in case there's any bother. If you could call me back it'd be much appreciated. Speak to you soon. Thanks, bye-bye.'

A reasonable period elapsed before Holly returned the call. Marvel was relieved and answered on the first ring.

'Marvel investigations Marvel speaking. How may I help?'

'What do you want. It's early and I'm tired.'

'I could do with your help'

'Does your personality need a refit?'

'No.' Marvel sighed. 'I'm working on an interesting case.'

'You realize you still owe me money?'

'Come again?'

'There's the matter of the segment of dance-floor from Paradise Garage you purchased? You still owe me cash for it. Or had you forgotten that you bought it from me?'

'I hadn't forgotten, no. Well, maybe. However, I figured I'm so kind, allowing you to tag along on all these cases you get involved in, you might overlook the final couple of payments from me.'

'Listen, Marvel, let's be clear on something, okay?'

'Okay.'

'I don't care if you have to resort to selling your body, for cash, in a public toilet, while wearing a toga, so long as you pay what you owe me. Incidentally, given that you owe me money and don't have the means to pay, what on Earth makes you think I'd be willing to help?'

''Oh, come on. Don't be like that. You like investigating crimes the old fashioned way. It's like a hobby, or an addiction—delete as appropriate. Plus, there's a grieving widow who's seeking closure, and you know you love a grieving widow, though in all honesty I get the impression she considered her hubby a waste of oxygen. Listen, I'll owe you a favor. You need me to chaperone you, I'll do it whenever, no strings attached, wherever you want to go. So, do we have a deal or not?'

There was a brief pause while Holly considered the proposal.

'Send me the coordinates before I change my mind. I'll be there in an hour. And this better be worth it, Marvel, or I'm turning around and coming straight back home again.'

'Deal.' Marvel smiled to himself, terminated the feed, and crushed the generic empty cardboard coffee cup he'd been sipping from into a tight ball before feeding it into the recycler.

They worked the scene in silence, a single story corner terrace in an abandoned residential district on the Salford Quays with the roof collapsed like a soufflé. Broken render and graffiti, plants sprouting from cracked and rusted guttering, the detritus of modern poverty strewn about, abandoned Smart tech, broken Memware products, food packaging and sex paraphernalia. It would be hard to find anything in this mess, even with Holly working the scene. It was a total ruin, the arse-hole of the city.

Unsurprisingly, the area had been marked for regeneration. What this meant was that 'affordable' Smart homes, with the latest AI embedded, would be coughed into existence for professional non-entities. The rents would be extortionate. Local families and the working poor would be priced out. Inevitably, they would be pushed to the city's periphery to facilitate the sanitation of their once thriving communities.

The house was one of a number of traditional terraced derelicts. On their arrival, Memware addicts stumbled out of the dusty hallway and down the front steps.

Marvel scouted about for a place to start.

'I'll check inside.' Holly said, thereby removing his decision-making responsibility. She gestured with her pretty brow at the gloom of the hallway ahead of them. 'You check out here. I'll be able to see inside better. If I find anything interesting, I'll text to let you know.'

Marvel deferred to the AI and began to browse the pavement surrounding the buildings, kicking rubbish aside, and parting the weeds to get a better view. There was no camera coverage here, he noted. No witnesses had come forward following the murder. It was possible someone saw what happened, but there was no point canvassing the transient population as anyone likely to have perceived events would have been zoned out on Memware and totally unreliable.

After twenty futile minutes of kicking down weeds, he received a message from Holly.

FOUND SOMETHING, COME C 4 URSELF.

Marvel entered the building and groped through the shadows while his eyes adjusted. Brick dust irritated his chest. He coughed his way into what was once a lounge area, tripping over the broken ruins of an antique computer monitor en route.

'Check this out,' Holly said. She opened her cupped palms to reveal the bagged up item enclosed within.

'What is it?' Marvel screwed his face in confusion. 'Is it Memware?'

'No, it isn't Memware. Trust me, I know what Memware products look like. There's a needle, see? Memware is uploaded via the brain stem. You have to have a port embedded to allow the connection. This is old school, clinical, an intramuscular injection device. I daresay it ought to appeal to your antiquated sensibilities, Marvel.'

'So what's it used for then?'

'I just told you. It's a device that is . . .was, used for injecting substances into muscle. You draw the substance into this plastic barrel and inject it into the muscle by depressing the plunger. There appears to be the remnants of a toxin of some sort inside, though I would need to analyze it to be sure what it is. One thing I can tell you, this has been used recently, there's blood on the needle where it's pierced the epidermis. No doubt you could get it checked against the victim, provided you have the DNA of the victim to hand.'

ORAL LOG OF SILAS MARVEL, RE: THE KILLING OF BRIAN WATERMAN IN MARCH OF THIS YEAR: STREAMING RESUME.

Bribe number 1:

A packet of the most expensive French cigarettes gets me into the mortuary where Holly scans the corpse, making use of her enhanced visuals to complete an analysis. She quickly identifies a puncture site behind the deceased's ear, the tiniest contusion, which wasn't recorded on the autopsy initially.

Bribe number 2:

Front row tickets to the Manchester derby at the weekend gets me a blood sample taken from the Clocker. Degradation levels are minimal. We return to the office where Holly can use the blood to complete a toxicology report. First up, the DNA matches that found on the needle. Also, it turns out the deceased had traces of a synthetic substance in his system when he died, TH1000, or some such, which Holly already identified as being the substance in the syringe. The substance, Holly informs me is used as a synthetic replacement therapy for ailing AI's. Over time, AI'S and occasionally clones have been known to suffer a rare blood disorder similar to the biological disorder of neutropenia, whereby their synthetic white blood cell count is inexplicably reduced. TH1000, another Anaphylaxis product, helps stimulate the production of white blood cells in AI's. The substance is benign when used by AI's and clones to combat the disorder, though it's toxic to biologicals, even in relatively small doses. As to why it didn't turn up on the original autopsy, it's not the sort of thing that would turn up on a routine blood test and could easily be missed unless a specific request was made prior to analysis to search for traces of it.

So, that rules the twins out. The Clocker was killed prior to initiating his cycle. The toxin and bloody syringe all but confirm this to be the case. The killing was faked to make it look like a gangland killing. An AI with a working knowledge of the twins' MO staged the murder scene. The twins didn't sanction the killing, any more than the AI who pulled the trigger was responsible. The question now is, who actually was responsible? Not the Clocker. It seems increasingly unlikely he was involved in the hijack. I'm still not sure whether he was the target or collateral damage.

Further investigation is indicated to establish whether this was the case or not.

What is more puzzling at present is how the Clocker's stop clock was triggered prior to his being cycled. How did the killer trigger the reset mechanism without the Clocker's password and vocal signature to initiate? The plot is surely thickening. I'll need some time to cogitate further.
STOP.

Marvel smoked a joint he had in his desk for mental emergencies such as this, leaning back on his chair with his boots up, considering the complexities of the case, which was puzzling to say the least, drifting into a psychedelic fugue state with his tongue lolling and head back. An hour later, mouth parched and neck aching from the unnatural angle he'd assumed while resting, he emerged once more into a state of semi clarity.

All roads led back to Harry. The killer, or killers could only have acquired the information they needed from one of two sources. Either the Clocker had told them, which at this point in the investigation was seemingly unlikely, or Harry the router told them, brain hot-wired to the AI, lie detector exonerated, punching his numbers and plotting maps, his consciousness plugged in like a cybernetic brain monster.

Marvel needed to search the router's brain, a relatively straightforward procedure involving a neurological software package of the sort Memware specialized in. He needed to sift the router's memories, to ascertain whether he had been tampered with recently. However, in order to enter the router's head and extract the information he required, Marvel needed leverage. Harry had passed the C + B test, which meant he believed his own innocence. If he had provided information, he had done so unwittingly. Thus he was never going to freely agree to an invasive cerebral procedure of the kind usually reserved for the complex synthetic brains of clones and AI's.

'I can hack his email,' Holly informed Marvel matter-of-factly the following morning. 'I can see if there's anything interesting there. I'm good at that sort of thing. It was a part of my original programming for the police.'

'You're eager to get into trouble all of a sudden.'

'It's an interesting case.'

'It's incredibly dangerous. You realize, of course, that it is highly illegal and you could face termination of the most appalling kind should you be caught with your fingers in this gentleman's trash folder?'

'Indeed. However, I doubt he's smart enough to catch me, to be honest.'

'Then do it . . . and for the love of God, keep it quiet. No footprints for him to follow. If he so much as gets a whiff there's something wrong, he'll wipe his system and go dark as black magic.'

Holly hacked the router's mail and dived into his trash folder, found what she was after, and quickly resurfaced. She uploaded her booty onto Marvel's system. Marvel ran through it, sordid correspondence with an anonymous recipient? Check!

'I believe we have our leverage.' Marvel chuckled. 'Have a look on the desk, Holly. The router's link up should be on there.'

'Found it!'

'Okay then, good. Let's give him a call, shall we? We'll invite him to dinner and confront him with his rottenness. Oh, and could you also get me a decent Memware package for the procedure? Mine's out of date. It could do with an upgrade. Also, just out of curiosity, is there any evidence the affair is ongoing at the moment?'

'None. Looks like it was ended a short while ago. The mails were deleted and he tried to wipe the folder. However, as you know, Detective, nothing can ever truly be deleted. With the right sort of eyes, everything is visible.'

Marvel approached the router again. He requested that he cooperate and engage in the procedure. The router refused the procedure categorically. Marvel fanned copies of the correspondence across his work desk.

The router, confronted with the damning details of his illicit liaison, and backed into a corner with limited room for negotiation, was initially outraged. Then he was frightened. Subsequently, his fear mellowed into acquiescence. After a short while, bubbling and simmering like stew, he agreed to the procedure and any subsequent questioning. In return, he requested they be discreet in their handling of the information, to reduce the chance of his wife finding out.

Marvel invited the router to his office. The procedure would take place the following morning. He was to have nothing to eat after midnight. He was to bring a decent book just in case he had to wait.

The following morning Wellens arrived promptly at nine.

'What are you going to do?' He inquired. He was less distracted than the first time they spoke.

'First, I need to check your brain for signs of tampering. After that, I may need to ask you some more questions. The procedure is quick. You might feel nauseous in the first instance, a bit of vertigo perhaps, but it's nothing to worry about. It's within normal parameters. However, if you start to feel your bowels loosen, that's a totally different matter.'

Holly rigged him with the appropriate enhancements. She uploaded the software to facilitate analysis. She ran the scan. Harry, meanwhile, vomited into a cardboard pot. A minute or two passed while the software did its thing. Harry continued to heave. Marvel continued to wait. Then, lo and behold, the scan was complete. Holly analyzed the results. Harry fell asleep. Marvel's patience began to falter. He drank coffee, ruminated, drank more coffee, and paced anxiously. Eventually, after a short period locked in her own head evaluating, Holly resurfaced. She smiled at Marvel and relayed her report.

'Harry shows all the signs of having been invaded neurologically, indicators of degraded nanotech in his bloodstream to facilitate control, blank spots in the cerebral cortex indicating redacted memories. This explains why he passed the lie detector test. He genuinely had no idea he'd been passing on information.'

EXTRACT FROM FURTHER INTERVIEW WITH MR. WELLENS REGARDING THE MURDER OF BRIAN WATERMAN IN MARCH OF THIS YEAR: STREAMING COMMENCE.

SILAS MARVEL: Okay then, if you would just like to state your name and occupation and relationship to the deceased for the record, we can commence with the interview.

HARRY WELLENS: Okay, so let me think . . . my name is Harry Wellens and I'm a router for Getters Inc. I was the router for the Clocker, Brian Waterman, also known as Safe Hands to those of us who knew him well, on the day that he was murdered.

PAUSE.

SILAS MARVEL: Okay, well, we'll start with the affair and go on from there. So, Mr. Wellens, what if anything, can you tell us about the lady alluded to in the correspondence retrieved from your trash folder?

HARRY WELLENS: Well, she was an AI for starters. She liked to be called Bobbi, which wasn't her real name. I agreed to go along with it. It was a harmless affectation.

SILAS MARVEL: And where did you meet Bobbi, the first time that you met her?

HARRY WELLENS: I met her in The White Horse, a pub in Castlefield. I go there sometimes, after work and at weekends. I like to watch the rugby and drink cider with the lads. She would sit at the bar on her own watching sports. We struck up a conversation. She was an excellent listener.

SILAS MARVEL: If we skip over the preliminaries, and assume you moved on from sports conversation to more intimate relations, did you ever meet up somewhere other than the pub?

HARRY WELLENS: She had a flat in Castlefield, near to the pub, a smart home she rented in the city. I would meet her there when my wife was at work. She would entertain, you know, dress up, play games, she would upload illegal Memware and we'd role-play different scenarios.

SILAS MARVEL: Do you have the address for us, Harry?

HARRY WELLENS: I can provide you the address, yes.

SILAS MARVEL: Anything about her physical appearance you recall? Remember what she looked like, any identifying features?

HARRY WELLENS: No.

SILAS MARVEL: It would seem, based on the evidence to hand, that she edited herself from your visual memory. She spiked you with nanotech and edited your recall. To put it more simply, what I'm saying is she seduced you, hacked your brain, and got you to tell her exactly what she needed about the Clocker and the route you planned, by controlling you with the nanotech, then she scrambled your head up so you wouldn't remember. Be grateful that's all she did. If my suspicions are correct, I'm surprised you're still alive.

HARRY WELLENS: Why didn't she kill me if you think she killed Brian. Why let me live and not tie up loose ends.

SILAS MARVEL: It's my humble opinion, Mr. Wellens, that in order to avoid any unwanted attention, she gambled on your silence, that your shame would be sufficient. Now is there anything else you can tell us about Bobbi?

HARRY WELLENS: There's one more thing, if you'll give me a moment.

SILAS MARVEL: Go on.

HARRY WELLENS: I received some images via my neural feed, a few days after she cut me off, black and white digitals that were seriously unsavory.

SILAS MARVEL: Did she make any demands?

HARRY WELLENS: She told me not to talk.

SILAS MARVEL: Is she visible on the images?

HARRY WELLENS: Mostly she's fuzzy.

SILAS MARVEL: Is there anything discernible?

HARRY WELLENS: The furniture and myself!

SILAS MARVEL: And you kept all the images.

HARRY WELLENS: Bizarrely, I retained them.

SILAS MARVEL: I need a copy of those images, Mr. Wellens, please mail them to Holly's neural feed. And thanks for your cooperation. You'll be hearing from us shortly.
STOP.

Wellens provided the stills, mailing to Holly's neural feed as requested. He exited the office, shuffling down Chapel Street quickly, barely a glance over his shoulder before crossing the road and disappearing into a sheet of spray thrown up by a passing bus.

'So what do we have?' Marvel asked on reentering his office.

'What we have is some aesthetically repellent, poor quality skin shots, black and white digital, not much to go on. What we don't have is Bobbi. Her face is never in the frame. When it is, her features are blurred or fuzzy or blank.'

'Okay, load them into the unit, lets project them round the room, I want to have a look and see if anything pops out.'

Holly sighed theatrically. She patted her empty belly.

'If you're genuinely hungry, there's Caribbean on the corner. And, if you don't fancy goat, there's the chip shop down the road.'

'Yuk!' Holly pulled a face at the thought of eating goat.

'Grab some coffee on the way too. I won't survive without a coffee. Get receipts for any purchases and I'll claim them on expenses.'

'Of course.'

She returned a half hour later, bearing coffee and jerk chicken. They ate while they worked, bobbing their heads to an Arthur Russell compilation. They pored over the pictures in minute detail.

They studied the stills, were frustrated by the lack of clarity, hunted out a bottle of half consumed Golden Trinidadian rum, swiped the stills to engage in a period of reflective meditation. Then, once the rum was gone and they were sufficiently well lubricated, they fell asleep, Marvel with his head on his desk and arm draped over his

Anglepoise, Holly on the chair opposite, with her feet resting on a crate of old records.

Around six, Holly shook his shoulder. Like most AI's she could enjoy the benefits of inebriation without any of the pitfalls of a subsequent hangover.

'Let's check the address he gave us. See if we turn anything up. She's pretty professional so it's likely there'll be nothing. We can get some breakfast en route, to help with your hangover. You can put it on expenses with the rest of your free shopping.'

ORAL LOG OF SILAS MARVEL, RE: THE KILLING
OF BRIAN WATERMAN IN MARCH OF THIS YEAR:
STREAMING RESUME.

The sun shone weakly through thin cloud and we walked to Castlefield, stopping at a greasy spoon for bacon sandwiches. The flat was a ground floor with no signs of camera coverage or a functioning AI and no evidence of any residents at home. The street was deserted so we hacked the lock and the apartment was empty - stripped, scrubbed, spotless, sanitized. We exited and returned to the office where we contacted the lettings agency as a last resort but they had no forwarding address for Bobbi and her details and references were faked. We tried to trace her IP address, just to be sure we couldn't locate her, but the address was bogus and impossible to track. So we had lunch and walked to the university and sat outside the museum while considering our options.
STOP.

'We appear to have hit a wall.' Holly said.
'Something will come up.'
'You don't sound convinced.'
'That's because nothing has come up yet.'
They loitered in silence for a moment. Neither of them could think of anything.
'What about the twins?' she asked.
'What about the lovely twins?'

'Perhaps we should approach them to see if they know anything. They probably know this Bobbi AI, and with the information we have, and the fact she tried to stitch them up by framing them for the murder, maybe they'd be willing to point us in the right direction. What do you think?'

'The twins are notoriously temperamental. I don't want to involve them if I don't have to. Don't want to owe them any favors. They're the kind of siblings who judge you based on what they can squeeze from you, not the sorts of people you want to be indebted to.'

'Fair enough. So what next?'

'Well, first of all, I'm going to eat a pie and smoke a joint and then I'm going to sit in the middle of my office and peruse those masochistic photos, just to be sure I'm not missing anything.'

'And then?'

'Then I report back to the widow. Tell her I've gone as far as I can go. Give her what I have and cash in my expenses.'

'Sounds grand! Well, that's me done for a couple of days anyhow. I'll leave you to it. I have some work I need to finish up. I'll catch up in a few days and see where you're up to.'

'Right e o then.'

'And don't forget. You owe me for this.'

Marvel smiled. He turned his back on the Salford museum, which was closed these days due to government funding cuts. He waved his hand at Holly. He hunched his shoulders against a temperature drop and slouched his way home. Turbulent skies broiled grimly overhead.

The next time they met was three days later on the Friday, outside a tattoo parlor in Lower Broughton, a part of the city mostly inhabited by AI's. It had been some time since the Clocker was murdered. It had been just over a week since the widow had retained Marvel's services. It felt like Marvel had finally made a breakthrough. The question now was whether anything would come of it, or whether it was another dead end like the flat had proven to be.

'So why are we here?' Holly asked, wrinkling her nose in distaste at the tattoo parlor shop-front.

'Cause I found something on the images that led me to this establishment.'

'You want a tattoo?'

'I don't want a tattoo, no.'

'Please elaborate then, cause I'm bored and it's chilly.'

'So, I went home the other day and messed with the photos again, like I said I would.'

'Was this after you had a pie?'

'This was after I had a pie, yes, and lo and behold, after a bit of tinkering and a couple of joints, I captured this image in one of the close ups.'

'What?'

'See this here?' Marvel pointed to one of the stills that he'd printed as a hardcopy. 'It's a tattoo. You see? Reflected in the background off the mirror on the dresser. Could be the AI's hip. I couldn't really tell. Anyway. It was only when I magnified and had it cleaned up that the image became sharper and I could see what it is.'

'And what is it exactly?'

'It's a dagger with a date on.'

'What's the date?'

'Some date a number of years ago, likely when she was initiated, cause that's what they indicate, sort of like a birthdate. Anyway, my point is, it's pretty unique.'

'How unique?'

'It's a signature burn and only one place in Salford does them. They're one of a kind, so they're simple to trace. The tattoo parlor specializing in these holographic tattoos, for militant AI's obsessed with their humanity, is none other than the reputable establishment we're presently patronizing.'

'Lovely.'

'Oh come on, admit it, you're a little bit impressed. Your eyes might be pretty, but you didn't notice that.'

'Whatever.'

Marvel chuckled. 'At the very least,' he said, folding the photo into his parka. 'It's provided me with a lead on the AI involved. With any luck, if we identify the AI as an accomplice, we can use her to finger whoever murdered the Clocker.'

'Okay.'

'You ready?'

'I'm ready.'

'We best go have a word then.'

ORAL LOG OF SILAS MARVEL, RE: THE KILLING OF BRIAN WATERMAN IN MARCH OF THIS YEAR: STREAMING RESUME:

The tattoo bloke, ex tap room attendant named Bernie, stick thin, darkly tanned, with muscles like old rope and a face like knotted tree bark, squinted at us myopically over the counter. You'll have to wait, he told us. There's coffee in the machine over there.

I asked the machine for a cappuccino. I'm sure it cackled before spitting a plastic cup out filled with lukewarm sludge. We waited in the reception area, surrounded by poor quality projections of Indian ink and holo burns. The room smelled of old smoke. There was a definite amber tinge reminiscent of inner city nicotine bars. The needle buzzed in the background. The proprietor provided the finishing touches to a vintage ink tattoo for a young clone lady with a shaven head, who smiled warmly at us as Bernie shifted the drapes.

A half-hour later Bernie emerged. He gestured for us to hand over the still. I flashed him my license to show I wasn't a con. He glanced at it cursorily before waving it aside. He recognized the holo burn immediately. It was definitely his work. There wasn't any doubt of it. It was a signature Bernie design. He projected a sales log. He checked to see who ordered the burn. He came back with details of an AI, Robert25Beat, a local businessman living in Lower Broughton who frequented the parlor for ink and holo-burns.

STOP.

'Let me get this straight,' Holly said as she scanned for Robert's address. 'Bobbi, the accomplice, is actually Robert?'

'Either that, or Robert, the accomplice, is actually Bobbi.'

'Indeed . . . Is it possible Bernie made a mistake?'

'He recognized the burn. He had the sale logged and signed for.'

'I suppose. And how would that even work?'

'Not sure. Don't get me wrong, I've heard rumors that the tech exists, illegally modified AI's and the like, usually prostitutes, high end models providing services via agencies, switching between genders, exclusive elitist perversions. Still, I always considered it to be nonsense.'

'No wonder.'

'Well . . . you learn something new every day, I suppose.'

Robert was no high-end agency doll, more like a services model gone rogue or let go. Still, that didn't mean he didn't have the mods. If he had the cash, somebody would be willing to provide him with upgrades. Anything was conceivable these days. With a big enough budget, the possibilities were endless.

'So what next then?'

'We probably need to tail the AI and see who he mixes with, see what he gets up to, accrue further evidence. He could lead us to the killer, although I seriously doubt it. Think he'll be keeping his head down until all this blows over. Still, at least we can tie him indisputably to the killing, that'll be progress, if we can gather more proof. Maybe then we can confront him with it. Who knows? He may roll over on his accomplice once the noose is round his neck.'

'Just so we're clear, you don't have a car. Come to think of it I'm not even sure you own a bike.'

'So?'

'So, you're paying for my car to be charged up, it'll save me the mileage and facilitate your stakeout.'

'Fine.'

'You take the first shift. I'll relieve you after work, and my car is clean so let's keep it that way, okay?'

ORAL LOG OF SILAS MARVEL, RE: THE KILLING OF BRIAN WATERMAN IN MARCH OF THIS YEAR: STREAMING RESUME.

Holly locates Robert, proud owner of a semi-detached Smart home in Prestwich, comfortable, nothing flashy, nice garden and decent views. I tail him for a day. Nothing suspicious occurs during the time I'm watching him. He owns a florist, works most days, Robbie's Roses, situated next to the Irwell on Frederick St, Works alone, arrives early, completes his orders in the morning, delivers them in the afternoon, returns home from work in the early evening, sleeps the night, gets up in the morning, starts the day over again.
STOP
STREAMING RESUME.

There's nothing to report day 2. The widow calls for a progress update. I fob her off until I have more proof. I eat pittas at a Greek cafe. Holly runs shifts with me to allow me to sleep a while to break up the monotony of relentless surveillance.
STOP
STREAMING RESUME.

Body odor percolates day three. Fast food cartons ripen. I spill coffee over the dashboard and dab at it with a napkin. I smoke a joint with the window open. I fart with the heater on. Inertia fattens my impatience. Raindrops finger tap the car bonnet relentlessly.
STOP
STREAMING RESUME.

He changes his routine day four, visits a local pharmacy, collects a prescription and returns to the florist. I contact Holly. I get her to hack the pharmacy records to

see what he collected. Holly sniffs at the security, out-of-date protection software and crumbling firewalls. She hacks it in minutes. She copies the relevant files, forwards her findings to my inbox. I read through them, a three-year summary of the florist's medical history. According to the files, the sexually androgynous Robert, who moonlights as a killer and has a penchant for azaleas, has a rare blood disorder particular to AIs. He receives a repeat prescription for it (TH1000 300mg/1ml) that he collects unfailingly on the last Friday of the month.
STOP
STREAMING RESUME.

Whoever killed the Clocker, prior to him being cycled, they're probably in the wind and unlikely to be apprehended. However, in spite of my skepticism, I shadow Robert again. Perhaps my luck will hold. He may yet provide me with a lead for the killer. I tail him from his flat in Prestwich. He drives to the Retek offices at the Salford Quays instead of the florist. I park a few cars down to avoid being detected. I observe the foyer of the building, confused by the change in his routine. The building, which is a textile warehouse converted to Retek's headquarters, is easy to observe from my present vantage point. I swill coffee. I rub condensation off the inside of the windscreen.

Half an hour later, the florist emerges, gets in his van and returns to the lower city. He commences a day of charity work. He ghosts the streets of AI slums, Patron Saint of Robotic Depredation, wandering the ghetto in the streaking rain, doling out kindness to the artificial masses. I observe him handing out meds on street corners, gifting AI components to discontinued work models. Memware products are distributed. Food and clothing are dispensed from the back of his work van.
STOP.
STREAMING RESUME.
While observing Robert's movements round the city, it occurs to me that my employer, the widow Waterman, who recently hired me to investigate the convoluted murder of her estranged husband, also works for Retek.

Now hold that thought a second while we consider the implications.

Could it be possible that the widow hired me to further exonerate her in the eyes of the law, having already misdirected the authorities with her charity gig alibi and the staged murder scene implicating the Burberry twins? In which case, perhaps hiring me was a ruse. Perhaps she hired me to safeguard her innocence, confident in the knowledge she would not be discovered?

What if the widow murdered her husband? What if she met this AI while working for Retek? She said it herself, her marriage was on the rocks, Brian slapped her around a bit, she no longer loved him, and everything was broken. What if she met Robert through her work, while she was most vulnerable, fell in love with him in his capacity as a pillar of the AI community, discovered his secrets, his androgynous sexuality and extra-curricular homicidal tendencies. Then, once she'd weighed up her options and realized they were limited, decided, given the recent boost in available resources, to thrash out a murder plan to jettison her husband?

It certainly solves one of the outstanding problems the investigation has encountered, namely how the password was acquired to trigger the Clocker's reset. If the widow was involved, she may have asked her husband for it when he was intoxicated. A more likely solution was that Robert was culpable. He may have infiltrated the Clocker's brain and extracted the password by covert means. Once they had the password, they would have no problem cloning a voice. All they would need was a recorded example of his speech. They could replicate the tone and pitch easily enough, and then modulate the content to facilitate activation.
STOP.

'It's always the woman,' Holly informs me nonchalantly. 'All the classics support this. The *femme fatale*, who presents as alluring and defenseless initially to deflect suspicion, turns out, beneath the veneer of vulnerable sensuality, she's a calculating killer with a heart made of stone.'

'Indeed.'

'That aside, you still have the problem of the alibi to address. If just the two of them were involved, how was she able to be in two places at once? How was she at the end of the route waiting to poison her spouse, whilst simultaneously at the charity event in a room full of witnesses? She was seen at the event. She talked to people there.'

'You ever hear of a golem?'

'I have heard of them, yes. Why?'

'What do you know about them, other than they're expensive to manufacture?'

'Well, I know for a sizeable fee, it is possible to have a clone of yourself constructed using DNA, black market Memware products, holographic imaging and reconditioned body parts. This clone – known as a golem on the black market, is operated via remote control. They were originally used in black ops by the military. However, they were expensive. Poor durability was an ongoing issue too.'

'Okay, we know golems are illegal. Not many people have the skill set necessary to construct one. You would need connections to acquire one and not just with the local Mcmware dealer either. We know Robert is well connected. We know he's resourceful. We know he has the cash. We know he cares for the widow. If he cares for her as much as we think, and given the lengths he's gone to assist—'

'Such as?' Holly enquired.

'Such as seducing the router and sifting his brain, providing his medication for use as the murder weapon, staging the final murder scene to make it look like the twins did it which only he would have been quick enough to do, then it's reasonable to assume he financed a golem. Now . . . assuming that to be the case, if it were used as a short-term intervention, depending on the quality of the workmanship involved, a decent golem would convince as an alibi.'

'You have any leads?' Holly asked.

Marvel grinned at her like a schoolboy. 'Well, I did a bit of digging while you were faffing at your day job, and spoke to a colleague of mine who works for the GMP.'

'Hang on a sec. Since when have you had friends on the GMP?'

'I have a lot of friends, in many different professions. I have friends in high places and friends in not so high places, such as yourself.'

'What did he say to you, this friend at the police?'

'According to my source, a well-known tech dealer by the name of Saul Mortimer was the most likely candidate. According to his file, he dropped off the grid recently to complete a custom order. He went underground. The police lost track of him.'

'So we locate the Golem maker and find out who hired him.'

'Police located him already.'

'And?'

'And if we want to communicate with him, to find out who hired him, we're going to need a medium to act as a go between.'

'Shit.' Holly shook her head in dismay.

'Indeed. Saul Mortimer was found murdered in a public toilet in London a week ago, shot twice in the back of the head while in the middle of taking a piss.'

'Do we know what happened to the golem?'

'It was witnessed leaving the event. Aside from that, however, we've no idea where it went. It would have needed to be stored somewhere, a garage maybe or rented lock up. As to where it is now, I suspect it's been disposed of. It was probably shot into orbit or discreetly incinerated to dispose of the evidence.'

'So what do we do next?

'We confront the AI, apprehend him, citizen's arrest and all that, wait for the police to show, hope that he rolls on his partner in the interim and take it from there.'

'And if he doesn't roll on her, what then?'

'We work Plan B into a viable alternative.'

ORAL LOG OF SILAS MARVEL, RE: THE KILLING
OF BRIAN WATERMAN IN MARCH OF THIS YEAR:
STREAMING RESUME.

*We confront Robert about his involvement in the killing
of the Clocker, and despite the fact Holly has a gun trained
on him to deter him from any rash course of action, he
somehow manages to break my nose. He incapacitates
Holly with minimal fuss and then dashes from the store into
the arms of a couple of juiced up thugs wearing holo-masks
and packing shotguns. Subsequently they bundle him into
a transit before fleeing the scene at high speed. All this
happens in the blink of an eye. I stem the blood spouting
from my nose with a ·bunch of synthetic daffodils. Holly,
meanwhile, scrambles on the floor in search of her missing
pistol. She eventually finds it, half in half out of a vase filled
with roses. She plucks it from the vase and stares at it
momentarily like she's disappointed in it for being removed
from her grasp. Then she replaces it in her holster.*

'Plan B?' she asks.

*'Plan B.' I confirm. I toss the flowers and pinch my
nostrils to stanch the loss of plasma.*
STOP
STREAMING RESUME.

*Less than twenty-four hours later, Robert is discovered.
His body is identified on the banks of the Irwell. His hands
and feet are bound with wire, blindfold soaked in bleach,
shot twice in the back of the head, both kidneys removed
via posthumous surgery.*
STOP.

Marvel had the mother of all headaches to contend
with, he was starting to develop panda eyes to compliment
his bruised and wadded nose, his cannabis stash had run
out and the painkillers he'd ingested were barely
efficacious. Also he was at a loss as to how to proceed. His
options were limited. The widow was in the clear unless
she confessed to her involvement.

'We call her bluff,' Marvel said suddenly. He thumped his fist against the desk. The Anglepoise wobbled and almost toppled over.

'Not to state the obvious, but your voice sounds stupid.'

'My nose is full of cotton. I'm bound to sound stupid. Now forget about my voice and let's focus on the strategy. We call her bluff. We tell her Robert confessed. We wait for her to crack and then we offer her a deal. Once she confesses to everything—in chronological order as befits a proper confession—we hand her over to the GMP.'

'And what if she doesn't crack up?'

'We could always beat it out of her in a windowless room.'

'Nice. But seriously, she was clever enough to get this far and probably would have got away with it, if not for the deductive acuity of Marvel Investigations Inc. What's the likelihood of her panicking at this stage?'

'Slim!' Marvel shrugged and then frowned his displeasure.

'We're going to need a better plan before we confront her. Let's face it, even if—and it's a big if at this point— Robert didn't implicate her before he was killed, it won't be much longer before she's running for the hills.'

'Okay, so, I think I have a plan worked out that's potentially doable.'

Holly eyed him suspiciously. 'How stupid is your plan on a scale of one to ten?'

'I reckon it's about a six, rounding to the nearest decimal.'

'Great.'

'Tell you what, we'll purchase some rum, have a drink, discuss the plan, thrash out any potential difficulties and problem solve them together. Then, if you still don't like it, we'll scrap the whole idea, approach the police, and hand over our findings. What do you say? You in or you out?'

Jane Waterman stuffed clothes into a suitcase and riffled through drawers, looking for cash she'd stowed and her passport. Robert was dead, kidnapped by the twins, butchered like cattle for his part in their frame up. The widow was afraid. This was despite her being certain that Robert had protected her. He would not have provided the twins with her identity. However, it only bought her limited time. It wouldn't be long before they sniffed out her involvement. Also, the detective was onto her. She could tell from his tone of voice. His reports were less frequent and the content of them was vague.

Her hair was glitching like crazy. The colour wouldn't settle at all. She sucked on her mood inhaler. The world was less frantic all of a sudden . . . And that was when the door to the flat burst open and two individuals wearing holo masks entered and she was pushed back and forced to sit in a chair with her hands tied and a gun against her head and she was told to confess how she met Robert and fell in love with him and how she organized the murder of her husband whom she hated and how they plotted her alibi and hired Marvel to sugar coat it and how they were going to wait a while and then leave the country with the money she received and Robert's blood money and live somewhere remote together for the rest of their lives and she begged them not to kill her she would do anything not to die and then the man holding the gun to her temple removed his mask and it was a woman and then the other person present removed his mask and it was Marvel and he held the recording of her confession and her hair went all the colors of the rainbow and he offered her an out by contacting the police and getting her into protective custody since there was no other way and she agreed to his offer and the police were contacted and she was taken into custody

EXTRACT FROM POLICE INTERVIEW WITH MRS WATERMAN REGARDING THE MURDER OF HER HUSBAND IN MARCH OF THIS YEAR:
STREAMING COMMENCE.

SGT. GATSBY: So, to summarize, Mrs. Waterman, you met the registered artificial intelligence Robert25Beat through your work with the Retek charity, correct?

MRS WATERMAN: That is correct, yes.

SGT. GATSBY: Did you know at that time that the flower business and his philanthropic community work was a front for his other work as a hired killer?

MRS WATERMAN: No.

SGT. GATSBY: When did you become aware of this?

MRS WATERMAN: Three months into the affair.

SGT. GATSBY: You didn't accidentally discover weapons in his basement or find incriminating evidence of some description that triggered a confession?

MRS WATERMAN: No.

SGT. GATSBY: Seems strange he would just tell you like that after such a short time.

MRS WATERMAN: Well there was no drama. It's up to you whether you believe that or not. We were in love, so when he told me about his work and the modifications he'd had done to convert to a woman, I accepted his explanation. People do worse things for money and since the people he murdered were bad people, it felt to me like a social service he was providing, rather than a criminal enterprise he was involved in.

SGT. GATSBY: When did you decide that you would murder your husband?

MRS WATERMAN: Not right away. We managed to keep our affair secret for a while, but then my husband found out about Robert, had us followed by some clone he hired to take photos of us together. He confronted me with the evidence one evening when he was drunk and we fought and he beat me and I ended up in hospital for my trouble. I was in the hospital with a broken jaw and fractured cheekbone, two fingers snapped, cuts and bruises everywhere. I asked him for a divorce, but there was no way he would provide me with one. In the end I started to feel trapped. I was afraid for my safety. Sooner or later he would seriously hurt me. Ultimately it was the logical choice. Either we put an end to my husband or his drinking and violence would put an end to me. Of course, organizing his demise required a rare amount of planning but since Robert could seduce the router to get us the information we needed, it was nowhere near as difficult as it might have been otherwise.

SGT. GATSBY: We know you infiltrated the router using an obscure form of nanotech.

MRS WATERMAN: We did. But what you don't know is that Robert seduced my husband too. Got him to bed, drugged him, extracted his password with the nanotech, used his weakness for leggy brunettes against him. He then redacted himself from his memory, safe in the knowledge that the devastation, wreaked by the post mortem gunshot wounds he inflicted, would make information retrieval impossible.

SGT. GATSBY: Why leave the router alive?

MRS WATERMAN: The router was problematic. Killing him would have aroused suspicion. We decided to judiciously edit his memory to maintain the illusion of the affair. The router was weak. We knew that his fear of the consequences of his affair becoming public knowledge would be sufficient to silence him. We partially redacted Robert from his memory as insurance against the possibility of the router having his memories trawled. This was to minimize the possibility of a positive ID in the event someone got to him. We left him with just enough recall to properly stoke his guilt. We blackmailed him, sent him some images to frighten and subdue him and we would have got away with it too, if Marvel had lived up to our expectations.

SGT. GATSBY: Did you commission the construction of a golem in your own image?

MRS WATERMAN: Robert did that.

SGT. GATSBY: And did you murder the engineer who constructed this golem?

MRS WATERMAN: Once delivery of the golem had been made and payment provided, Robert hacked his accounts. We cleaned him out. Then we killed him to maintain his silence.

SGT. GATSBY: Did you poison your husband?

MRS WATERMAN: I poisoned him with Robert's medication. I injected him with the TH1000 and watched as he died, his legs kicking, soiling himself like an animal. Then I cycled him using the password Robert had retrieved.

Robert finished the job and staged it to look like a gang killing.

SGT. GATSBY: One more question.

MRS WATERMAN: Ask as many as you like officer.

SGT. GATSBY: Why hire a private investigator to look into the death of your husband when it seems to me as if you'd managed to get away with it?

MRS WATERMAN: The plan was to improve our cover, but I suspect it was partly hubris on my part looking back. The police investigation was questionable. We had faith that our ruse would dupe the detective. Ultimately, we wanted to strengthen our position.

SGT. GATSBY: Well that'll be all for now, Mrs. Waterman. This concludes the initial part of the interview. Interview terminated at 14:30 on the date already specified.

STOP.

'So,' Marvel sighed, over velvety coffee the following week, when they met up to debrief in the offices of Marvel, Inc. 'that's another case solved. It's back to cheating husbands and teenage runaways for me. I'll let you know if anything interesting comes up. In the meantime, let's see what you make of my earworm of the day.'

Marvel hit the PLAY button on the Hi Fi system.

'Pause it.' Holly said.

'Why?'

'I have a question.'

'What question?'

'What's an earworm?'

'Are you serious?'

'As a death certificate.'

'Alright then.' Marvel hit the PAUSE button. He considered his response. 'An earworm,' he began mulling over his words carefully, 'is a figure of speech used to describe what it's like when a tune gets in your head and stays there for days and you can't get it out no matter how hard you try.'

'Does it hurt?'

'Does it heck!'

'Sounds painful.'

'Well it's not.'

Marvel hit the PLAY button. Holly hit the PAUSE.

'What now?' Marvel was getting exasperated.

'This tune.'

'What about it?'

'It's rubbish.'

'It's a classic.'

'It's annoying.'

'You're annoying.'

'Like an earworm?'

Marvel huffed his frustration. 'I'll have you know that Prince Rogers Nelson was a musical genius. He was a consummate bandleader and an inimitable showman. He never compromised his art, not even for the big record companies. Also, he somehow managed to blur the boundaries between race and gender to the point of redundancy. To round it off, he was a top-of-the-line six-stringer. I mean seriously, what's not to like?'

Holly shrugged. Marvel ejected the CD. He finished his coffee and patted her on the shoulder. 'Your turn to pick! I'm off to the deli. A double espresso to combat my fatigue.'

'Time for me to go,' Holly said. 'Wait and I'll come out with you.'

Marvel waited. Holly exited the office. He gave her a hug and told her he'd call her if anything worthy popped up. Then she turned, waved over her shoulder, stepped into the street, and was gone towards the city. Marvel observed her departure. He waited until she reached the junction. Then he buttoned his jacket, flipped up his collar, placed his hands in his pockets, and set a course for the deli.

In the future, being unhealthy is outlawed. Eating meat is a crime punishable by death. Underground dinner parties are on the increase, though for Annabelle Jones the consequences of attending could prove disastrous.

VEGAN STATE

I attend my gym session in the morning, though when the alarm on my phone goes off I seriously consider throwing it across the room. I have a lukewarm shower, inject breakfast and get dressed. Then I make the journey on an antique bicycle. My petrol allowance has been used up. I'm unable to use my scooter to travel until next month. I can't afford a hydro-car. Once the monthly fuel ration is gone, the bicycle is my only mode of transport.

Gym sessions are three times a week. I log in at the door. This is to prove I attended. I place my ID in the mouth of the gym bot. Its eyes flash red. It begins to talk to me. This is around a mouthful of ID plastic.

'Welcome to The Fitness Hub, Anabelle! Please acknowledge previous non-attendance!'

I reach forward to remove my ID. There's a queue forming behind me. I glance over my shoulder to apologize. A cretinous ogre is ogling my arse.

I remove my card and yank the receipt from the bot's mouth—a 50-credit fine the day before payday! The scanner debits my account. I check the receipt, which updates my infringements. Skipped meals, dodged gym sessions, failure to recycle appropriately, accumulated illness. There's a notification in small print. If I fail to comply with my life plan, if I dodge a gym session or forfeit a carrot soup at meal times again, I will have to attend a hearing. A hearing will mean an investigation. I will be scrutinized. My private life will be under the microscope.

41

That is unacceptable. Given the kind of company I've been keeping, the sort of social life I've been enjoying lately, the last thing I need is the state paying attention to me.

Health fascism is trending. It is an age of enforced vigor. Unhealthiness is outlawed. Fitness is mandatory. It's the middle of the century and boredom is endemic. You can't have sex without a license. An illegal pregnancy carries a mandatory ten-year sentence. Dietary laws are ridiculous. The penalty for eating meat is a mandatory life sentence.

I met Carly St John by chance one night. We were attending a music event in the city; the only drinks available were organic juice. Health officers monitored the event. All music events are monitored like this in the city. There are occasionally substances on offer, though dealers are reluctant to trade due to the penalties incurred if they happen to get arrested.

I was seated in a chill out area where the music was ambient. I was having a breather away from the lights and blazing music. Carly and her friends were seated nearby. Carly, with her 10% body fat and bioluminescent skin, was watching me intently.

After a while she gestured me over. Disinhibited Carly, under the influence of something, taking me into her confidence, seducing me with her pheromones. We began to discuss the government and meat and how I'd not eaten meat since I was five years old.

'Would you like to?' She asked a tad flirtatiously.

'Be serious.' Nervousness made my voice crack.

'I am.' She put her arm round my shoulder and continued to murmur in my ear.

I felt like I was part of something; like the French resistance fighters during the great war of the last century. She told me she would be in touch with further details, though I promptly forgot about the invite and went about my day-to-day activities as if we'd never even spoken.

That was a year ago. Since then I've attended a number of dinners, spread across the North West. Carly and her friend Eve arrange them. Another associate, a chef by the name of Barney procures the meat and prepares the menu. It's a very select group of foodies that attends; a zealous, well-organized bunch more interested in Beef Wellington than kick-starting a revolution. Still, with the government clampdown on illicit dinners in force, I wonder how long it'll be before we're shut down.

It's the first Saturday of the month. I've been off work for the last week, relaxing and forgetting to attend to my life and health plans. I used to be a good civilian. I used to adhere to all the rules and regulations. That changed when I met Carly. It changed for good when I tasted my first kebab.

There's a dinner planned for later this evening. A couple of regulars have sent their apologies. They are unable to attend due to work and family commitments. There will be eight diners in attendance. They will be sent a text prior to the meal. This will be sent two hours before service. It will inform the diners of the event's location. There will be directions for those not familiar with the area.

I finish my evening meal, and then I sign for it on my computer. I dim the lights in my crappy apartment, with the busted sofa and empty fish tank and the gas fire and the temperamental dishwasher. I put on my headset, upload a pirate radio transmission from The Chef, self proclaimed voice of the disenfranchised and unhealthy, listen to him for a while, ranting about the recent increase in government fines for obesity and other health plan infringements. Then, when I can no longer stand the tedium and my eyes are closing and I no longer think I'm going to get the call, I receive a text via my headset.

I forward the text to my computer. Once I've decoded the missive, (all communication is encrypted since interception by the wrong person could cause a lot of trouble,) I scribble the address on a bit of foolscap. I delete the message. I get changed and rush my shower due to there being a water shortage this month. I wear a dress and heels and grab a coat on my way out; this is in case it goes cold later on. I hail a rickshaw and commence my journey. The meal is to be served in an abandoned hall. The hall was once an old lad's club in Walkden. According to the text, the hall is a solitary building near to woodland and will serve admirably as a cantina for the night.

I arrive at the hall thinking I'll be first. However, Maria Carter, with her beehive and black chiffon dress, her perfect make up and designer cigarettes, has arrived ahead of me. Her beehive is slightly wonky. Her hands are fidgeting nervously with her bag strap.

Maria sees me. She fixes her smile in place. She rights her beehive. Her hands become still. She gestures me over. She's slightly older than me, somewhere in her mid-thirties. She's an extremely elegant lady with a taste for fine dining. She greets me as I draw near. She puts her arm through mine and we enter the building together like sisters meeting for brunch.

The foyer smells of damp. There's mold on the ceiling. It's dank and unseemly and radiates neglect. Not the most auspicious start I think. I cough due to the plaster dust I inhaled as we entered.

After a moment of loitering with neither of us commenting, Maria smoking a cigarette and me picking my fingernails, the grand doors leading to the hall - the only handsome feature we've encountered thus far, are opened from within and Carly steps forward.

Carly, looking as ageless and spectral as a Victorian ghost child, dressed in a luminescent wraparound and wearing contact lenses that make her eyes shine, ushers us into the hall. Nobody speaks. The moment is a magical one. The hall has been theatrically lit. Variably sized candles flicker and dance. It's a complete contrast to the foyer, which was a shudder inducing derelict. The hall is clean and romantic, permeated by cooking smells, warmed by a log burner that crackles in the fireplace.

We attend our seats, which are identified through name cards. I order a glass of red wine and await the starter. The other diners arrive after us and take their places around the table.

The menu is as follows:

Fois Gras toasts served with a fig chutney and salad, followed by a mixed game pie served with roasted seasonal vegetables. Finally, dessert is a white chocolate torte served with raspberry coulis.

It's a wonderful meal, cooked to perfection. The company and conversation is excellent. I feel relaxed and sated. Any nervousness I may have been feeling has been dissipated by the food and wine.

Everything is running smoothly, like clockwork. It's during dessert when it all turns to shit. The doors to the hall explode off their hinges. Carly who is closest to the explosion, is flung sideways out of her chair. A jagged wooden shard protrudes from her throat. She crumples in a heap on the sanded wooden floor. Blood jets up the wall behind her, rendered doubly grotesque by rifle-mounted torch beams.

NOBODY MOVE. EVERYBODY DOWN. EVERYBODY DOWN. DOWN ON THE FLOOR NOW! DON'T MOVE MOTHERFUCKERS. DOWN NOW! GET DOWN. HANDS BEHIND YOUR BACK...

I exit through a window in the confusion. I manage to get out unnoticed. I stumble into an officer guarding the perimeter as I jump down from a window ledge. The officer dodges. He tries to club me with his Taser but hits the wall instead jarring the Taser from his grasp. This gives me enough time to take advantage by retrieving it and firing it into his chest. The noise from the house muffles the sound of our encounter. This enables me to limp from the madness, under cover of darkness into the woodland nearby. I wait for the chase to commence, but nobody comes after me, which is just as well given I've been temporarily deafened and my ankle hurts where I twisted it escaping.

I withdraw as much money as possible following the ambush. I know that my accounts will soon be frozen.

I wonder what my next move will be. What happens once the money runs out? I will have to leave the country, but first I need shelter.

I quickly go to ground. I take a room in an anonymous hotel. It's the sort of place criminals and prostitutes frequent. People's faces blur when you try to focus on them. Convenient I think, given I'm wanted for eating meat and assaulting an officer of the law. I download podcasts and pick up radio transmissions from The Chef. I think of Carly. I wonder how the police managed to find out about the party. I turn it over in my head, over and over, piecing events together such as who the guests were, what was the seating arrangement? Where was everybody when the door was blown? Was anybody behaving oddly in the run up to the police arriving?

I try to remember who was missing when the door was blasted. Carly and Eve seated at the head of the table furthest away from me, a bloke called Darren who was relatively new to the right of them. Barney had come in from the kitchen and was seated opposite trying to converse with Darren. There was Robert the librarian with his tie askew. His wife Blossom, from Spain, was also present. Finally, there was Maria and myself, Maria with her relentless chatter, talking about pork and jogging and perfume.

I visualize the hall. The person missing when the door was breached was Maria. She'd gone to use the bathroom. She was the only one of us not present. Before the meal, I think, when I met her outside she looked uncomfortable, flustered and anxious.

The question now is what do I do next? Make a bid to get to safety or attempt to confront Maria. I know where she lives. I've been there before. Planning meals and meetings. Composing menus. Think! What would Carly have done under the circumstances?

I check the streaming news and journals and find myself in a number of the dailies, grainy black and white from my student days, mug shot taken at a local health office, breach of the peace, something like that, demonstrating against government cuts. Now I'm accused of attacking an officer during a dinner party. Not very flattering, I think, and I clearly forgot my make-up.

Officer Attacked!

Officer Damien Ripley, aged 25 from Monton was attacked and grievously injured after responding to an illegal dinner party in Walkden at the weekend.

Officers were called to the scene at a building in Walkden after reports from neighbors of suspicious activity.

Annabelle Jones of 51 Chapel St is being sought for questioning in connection with the attack. A local resident positively identified the waitress on a nearby street following the incident. Colleagues at The Lentil Palace restaurant, where Jones had recently been working, were shocked to hear of Miss Jones' involvement in illegal dining.

Miss Jones was due to return to work this Monday after a week off. However, she has yet to report for duty. Neither friends nor family can confirm her whereabouts at this time.

Seeing my photo splashed over endless web pages and news items explodes my paranoia. I purchase a blonde wig, glasses, and sandals. I dress poor, ripped jeans and a winter coat purloined from a washing line that makes me look muscular. I sit in a launderette across the street from Maria's flat. I watch for a few days and observe the comings and goings. No officers enter or leave. Nobody looks out of place. There are no uniforms. There are no cameras covering the alley. I may have missed something. It could be a trap. Or perhaps, and this is the more likely rationale, they believe I've made a run for it and am no longer in the city. Perhaps they underestimated me? In doing so they've provided me with a clear run to the traitor who sold us out.

I exit the launderette. I cross the road and duck into the alley in back of the flats. I loiter there for a while, taking cover behind some empty crates. I wait for a resident to come out to dump trash. It isn't long before my patience is rewarded. An athletic thirty-year-old man pushes the door open. A tanned arm swings a bag of refuse into a Biffa bin. He lingers for a minute and checks there's nobody about. He snatches a couple of puffs on a cigarette. The minimum sentence for smoking is a two-month custodial, a fortnight of rehab and a three hundred credit fine. Chuffing smoke, he flicks the cigarette in my general direction. The lit fag end fizzles out in a puddle. The door eases closed behind him. Once he's out of sight I step from my hiding place and follow him in. He doesn't notice me. I wait until he's entered his flat. I listen for any residents on the stairs. Then I head up the stairwell. Maria's is the only apartment on the third floor. I check the door and find it unlocked. I step into the flat, the smell of environmentally friendly polish back drafting as I enter. I pull the door closed after me and await her return.

The flat is minimally furnished. No character. Mismatched furniture and hardwood floors. The centerpiece of the lounge is a bespoke coffee table. This is made of pine with an ornamental sundial protruding from its center.

I crouch beside a lampshade with oriental writing on it. I await the arrival home of the woman responsible for my friend's death. My patience is rewarded a couple of hours later. The front door opens and closes. There is a bit of shuffling, a coat and shoes being removed, a bag being dropped.

Following this, Maria floats into the living room, borne up on a cloud of perfume. It precedes her into the lounge, informing me of her presence. On entering the room, Maria claps twice. The lamp beside me casts my shadow across the coffee table. She's dressed in an expensive sheathe dress. Her long auburn hair flows down over her shoulders. She freezes on seeing me. Fear creases her features momentarily. She stares at me for a moment. Neither of us says anything.

After a moment I break the silence.

'Why did you do it?' I ask.

'For the money,' she says.

'How much?' I ask.

'Enough,' she says. Her smile is a crimson slash. It opens her face up like an ugly knife wound.

'Carly's dead,' I tell her through gritted teeth.

'So what?' she shrugs. She flicks her hair like she's auditioning for TV.

Then she rushes me. The plan was to tackle me I think, like a rugby player. In her haste she trips over the couch. Shock widens her eyes. Her hands come up to protect her face but they're no protection against the coffee table with the fake sundial protruding from its center which pierces her left eye socket and kills her instantly. I stare at the point of the sundial protruding from the back of her head. I have time to wonder at the brain and scalp stuck to it. There's mess everywhere. I step away from the demolished coffee table to avoid the blood reaching my sandals.

I search the flat quickly for any valuables she might have stashed. I hit the jackpot when I find a makeup bag stuffed with credits in her underwear drawer. I retrieve an overnight bag from under the bed and fill it with dresses and clothing. I'll get changed before I leave, she was about my size, should be okay. I'll steal a hydro car and skip town. I'll head for the hills using the B roads. I'll lay low for a while and hope it all blows over. Maybe they'll find me. Or maybe I'll be safe.

Before I leave I stuff a credit note in Maria's mouth. I rummage in her handbag and come up with a red lipstick. I use it to scrawl a bloody message on the bedroom mirror.

RIP Carly St John.

I ease out of the flat. I make my way down the stairwell. I slip out of the fire exit. I pause in the alley. I anticipate arrest for a moment, amplified voices shouting, the sound of shots fired, a storm of bullets, a violent death. The only sounds are those of a plane overhead. I stare at it a moment. I watch until it vanishes. I adjust my sunglasses and then step out of the alley.

Vegan State was first published in Perihelion Online Science Fiction Magazine (July 2014).

A giant asteroid is on a collision course with the Earth. Armageddon is imminent. However, some people will go to any lengths to avoid the pending apocalypse.

(225-50) AGNES

In an unprecedented joint international address, the world's government's announced to the planet that doomsday was imminent. An asteroid by the name of (225-50) Agnes would devastate the planet's surface in approximately three years. In order to appease the world's population and to avoid a catastrophic panic, it was quickly highlighted that though the world was doomed. and everything on the surface of it, steps had been taken to safeguard the species. A broadcast to the public would be forthcoming in no less than 6809 languages worldwide to illustrate how this was to be achieved in more detail.

It was my thirty fifth birthday. I was unmarried. I didn't have any kids. My parents were both dead. I was incredibly rich. Not only had I inherited a shit load of money from my super wealthy parents, but my work as one of the foremost investment bankers in the world had been lucrative, to say the least. I could afford anything I wanted, with the exception of the thing I wanted most, which was a place on the Ark Europa. I'd tried blackmail, bribery, intimidation, offering people vast sums of money to part with their tickets, all to no avail. Unfortunately, I couldn't acquire one no matter what I attempted. It had become apparent to me that those who were lucky enough to be allocated places on the Ark, and those who had won them during the weekly lottery these last couple of years, were unwilling to part with them. I found this strange, initially. I used to believe everyone had a price. Having said that, if it was me faced with the choice of a lifetime as an interstellar Bedouin or as a mole in an overcrowded subterranean bunker, I know what I'd have opted for every time.

The black market surgeon who reconstructed my face was stabbed to death in a brutal mugging that took place in a public toilet days after the surgery was completed. Said surgeon was stabbed fifteen times in all before he eventually bled to death in a toilet cubicle with his head resting against a toilet roll dispenser.

> *A thirty-year-old man, living in the Merseyside Area, has today come forward to claim the final lottery prize of a place on the Ark Europa. The Ark Europa, which has finally been constructed following a number of delays and setbacks, caused by engineering and construction difficulties, is now awaiting its eventual ascension. It is scheduled for lift off precisely eighteen months from now and has finally reached its full capacity. There will be no more lottery winners.*
>
> *'I am over the moon,' said Gerald Braithwaite during an interview with the media at the shop where he bought his ticket. 'I feel privileged to have been given this opportunity to represent Earth on the Ark's ascension.'*
>
> *Meanwhile the rest of the earth's inhabitants prepare to go underground as the final preparations are made to gradually evacuate the surface of the planet.*

Initially I was optimistic, though as the weeks went on and my name wasn't called, I began to feel cheated. Then suddenly there were no more winners to be had. Time, it would seem, was officially running out.

I did a bit of research after it became common knowledge the earth was done for. What I came up with, or what I could fathom from all the jargon, due to my not being a sci-fi nerd or a world leading astro-physicist, was the following. Agnes was probably an NEA (Near Earth Asteroid) whose elliptical orbit of the sun within the asteroid belt between Mars and Jupiter had been altered, after it had gotten too close to Jupiter or one of the other big asteroids, and been thrown across space into a collision course with Earth. Agnes was a mile-long piece of space rubble. She was an acne scarred, potato shaped, S-Type asteroid composed mainly of silicate and nickel iron. It was estimated that she would impact the earth at about thirty thousand miles an hour. This was the equivalent of an impossibly monstrous bomb going off— what was known as an extinction event. Essentially, what it meant for humanity was that we had to vacate the premises long enough to allow the dust to settle or dig a hole deep enough to hide out underground until the all clear was given.

I'd spent the evening with a prostitute in a swanky hotel in the country. It was three in the morning. I was snorting coke off one of her thighs. I got a nosebleed and had to go to the bathroom to clean up. While I was there, sitting naked on the toilet with my head back and a courtesy towel clutched to my face to stopper the blood, I had my epiphany. I was thinking about the last winner, Braithwaite, or whatever his name was, and suddenly it hit me. I would become Braithwaite. I'd heard about the wave of identity frauds sweeping the continent. People were being arrested weekly for assuming other's identities. Often they were discovered because their surgeries were botched, the retinal work was poor, the DNA didn't match up and that sort of thing. However, I had inexhaustible funds. I could afford to have the work done properly. All that I needed was the model on which to base myself. There would be complications, and there would be a clean-up involved after I was done being enhanced. Still it would be worth it if I pulled it off, since I would be one of the lucky few chosen by fate to embark on The Goldilocks Endeavour.

The World's government's had known about Agnes for some time. Unbeknownst to the planet's denizens, with the exception of those involved in the projects (sworn to secrecy on pain of death), they'd been preparing for the inevitable these last two decades.

First up was The Ark Project, a collaborative venture involving most of the world's nations. A couple of countries had abstained, choosing instead to participate in the

Bunker Initiative, more of which later. The Ark Project was being touted as a cosmic reimagining of Columbus. The idea was that mankind, or a designated portion of it at any rate, would embark on an epic interstellar journey, The Goldilocks Endeavour, as it came to be known, in search of a new planet to colonize, somewhere in deep space. Ark naming rights would go to the sponsor Somy, or one of the other big software companies to be announced at a later date.) The Arks were mega-sized space vehicles capable of housing, in relative comfort, millions of inhabitants. Capable of recycling oxygen and growing their own crops, they were a staggering feat of engineering. Hats off to whomever it was had conceived of them. Their size alone was unimaginable. In fact, they proved so unbelievable initially that some people were querying whether the revolutionary propulsion system, among other things, used to propel them on their way, was made of alien technology salvaged from a UFO crash.

The woman who created and inserted my eyes and calibrated my voice box to sound like Braithwaite, crashed off a bridge into a fast moving river. The brakes on her sports car failed to engage. She was knocked unconscious as the car hit the water and drowned in her seat as the car submerged.

I read all the articles about the last winner, over and over, committed his face to memory and researched his history. I began to ruminate and obsess over him. I was constantly cogitating. How was it, I thought, that some shit heel who has leeched off the state all his life and snubbed his nose at every opportunity, gets to escape the coming apocalypse. Meanwhile, men like myself, who have worked and sweated all their lives and earned their wealth —a good proportionate of it at any rate—through blood and hard graft, have been condemned to crawl under the ground like insects?

Second up was The Bunker Initiative. This, in theory would provide a place of safety below the Earth's surface for the multitudes of races remaining on the planet. A number of bunkers had been constructed. They were self-sufficient with the capacity to support millions of people for well over a century.

The religious nuts are having a field day with Agnes. On my way home today I observed, scrawled on the side of a bridge on the way in to Manchester, 'And the meek shall inherit the earth.' It was cheerfully rendered in looping pink neon. It was as if the artist who composed it was actually optimistic. I find such optimism delusional at best. My guess is that once Agnes hits, there won't be much left for the meek to inherit.

The Arks were oversubscribed. In order to allocate the remaining places on them, once you'd factored in all the scientific and engineering folk and the flight crew and medics and farmers and biologists and other necessary folks, it was decided to use a lottery. Millions of names would be input into a huge database. A random draw would take place weekly. If your name came up, you would be offered a spot. If you refused, your place would be reallocated in a subsequent lottery.

In order to become Braithwaite and take his place on the Ark, I would have to get samples of his hair. I would have to have his retinas scanned and have my own eyes replaced. I would have to undergo an excessive number of facial surgeries, my voice box would need re-calibrating, my fingerprints would need burning off to be replaced by biologically replicated skin grafts. I would also need to observe his routines, to know what time he gets up, who he associates with, how he talks, his hobbies, whether he smokes, what bars he frequents, what food he likes, and all manner of things. Most of this could be done through observation and surveillance. I would have cameras set up covertly in his home. I would have him followed and the details reported back daily.

Humanity's response to the disaster was surprising. Instead of panicking, as was the general expectation, the people of Earth embraced Armageddon. Knowing what they knew, that they were potentially safe from the pending desolation, it was suddenly an event that everybody looked forward to. The corporations typically saw it as an opportunity. They exploited the world's end with an impressive array of products. Games companies released holographic 3D simulations and first person shooters to cash in on the Asteroid craze. Fast food companies released apocalyptic tie-in meals and Asteroid burgers. Brands began to compete over who would sponsor the Ark project. Who would provide the highest bid? Who would have their company's logo distributed throughout space? Conspiracy theories began to circulate that Big Business had engineered the asteroid's arrival to boost flagging profit margins in collaboration with the world's governments. Construction companies were already bidding over redevelopment contracts for when the surface of the Earth was inhabitable again, just like when Hurricane Katrina hit all those years ago—disaster capitalism on a cosmic scale.

I found myself wondering, what if he expired before I was able to complete my metamorphosis? How would I explain myself to people? How would I explain my appearance? What reason could I give for my sudden transformation? I began to hurry things along a bit. I learned where he went during the day, how he spent his free time, the fact he didn't have anyone who was close to him. That was something at least. When I assumed his identity, I wouldn't have to convince his friends and family who I was. He did not have any after all. He did not have a wife or children. He had no brothers or sisters, and none of his parents were above ground. At least we had something in common, I thought. That was one part of this idiot's life I wouldn't have to fake.

Meanwhile, leaders of the world's great and not so great religions began to vocalize about God's Wrath. As it turned out, they were quite excited about the prospect. The end of the world vindicated their beliefs. It wasn't long before they began to argue over whose God was responsible. As it turned out, everybody wanted it to be his or her God swinging the wrecking ball, as opposed to the lesser deity of an inferior faith.

I thought of a number of elaborate ways to get the samples I needed from Braithwaite. In the end I settled for the simplest route available. I decided to kidnap him. I snuck up on him one night in a car park close to where he lived. I chloroformed him with a bit of old cloth, bundled him into a van, and drove him to an abandoned warehouse on the outskirts of the city. I took a cast of his head while he slept. I scanned his retinas. I took hair samples and nail samples, skin samples, and blood samples. Then I tied him to a chair in a room. There was nothing in the room except for a speaker system for me to communicate with him and a computer monitor for him to read my instructions. I got him to read a number of different sentences, which I needed to be able to have his voice cloned. Then, once I'd gotten what I needed from him, and I'd roughed him up and stolen his wallet to authenticate the kidnapping, I abandoned him on waste ground near to a train station in Cheshire.

> *In other news today, the universal Ark project will be fully boarded and loaded up this week, ready for ascension in four weeks' time. Notice has been given to those lucky enough to embark on the flight, in what has now become known as The Goldilocks Endeavour.*
>
> *The five Arks: Ark Europa, Ark America (nicknamed the Mayflower 2), Ark Asia, Ark Russia, and Ark Australasia, will set off on a mission, potentially spanning centuries, to find a planet similar to the Earth.*
>
> *Meanwhile in other news, a religious group calling themselves the Sons of Forever, and numbering, according to some estimates as many as one million members worldwide, have today announced that they will be remaining on the earth's surface for the coming event, in order to face God's Judgment together. More on this story as it continues to unfold.*

I saw myself in the mirror once the facial surgery and shaping was completed, my voice had been changed and my eyes and fingerprints. I was immediately disorientated.

My God, I thought. Who am I? I'm not who I thought I was. I'm not who I think I am. What happened to me? Where have I gone?

I ran into the bathroom and vomited, turned the shower on, and stepped under the freezing water. I cried for a while, curled up on the floor, veering between a potential psychotic episode and insight into my predicament. Gradually, as the shock wore off I started to calm down a bit. My name is Braithwaite, I kept telling myself over and over like a mantra. My name is Gerald James Braithwaite.

The young gay couple that sorted my fingerprints out for an impossibly extortionate sum—confidentiality guaranteed—were killed in a house fire caused by faulty electrical wiring. There was no trace of an accelerant when the fire was investigated, but then great pains were taken to make sure foul play was not suspected.

When the day came to take Braithwaite's place I attended his home and rang the front doorbell. As I waited for him to answer, I was remarkably calm. When he opened the door and saw his doppelganger smiling back, it must have come as a bit of a shock. I pushed him into the house at this point and removed the pistol from inside my jacket. I'd attached the silencer a few moments ago in the car on the way over. I shot him twice in the chest. He fell away from me and sat down with an expression that was part pained, part surprised. He turned to crawl away. There was a sticky blood smear along the floor and I stepped around him. I pressed the silencer-muzzle against his skullcap and shot him once more in the back of the head. His head jerked forward. Brain and bone spattered the tiled hallway. His feet kicked. I watched dispassionately as his body convulsed.

'Ark Europa, you will be cleared for ascension in T Minus ten seconds and counting. Nine, eight, seven, six, five, four, three, two, one, Ark Europa you are cleared for takeoff . . .'

It was a couple of seconds before I noticed we were not alone. A young black woman with a sheet clutched to her chest to hide her nakedness was crouched trembling against the wall to my right. Tears streamed from her eyes. I stared at her a moment. No witnesses, I thought. I pointed the gun. It clicked to indicate it was jammed. I tossed it onto the floor. The woman ran. I immediately gave chase. She ran up the stairs across the landing into the bathroom. She tried to lock the door to prevent me from entering. I shoulder charged it open. I accelerated toward her. We tumbled into the bath together. She screamed and hit out blindly. I pulled the shower curtain down and tightened it around her throat. I proceeded to strangle her with it. Her eyes popped as I strengthened my grip. Her mouth worked silently. Her face turned beet red. Her feet kicked furiously against the bath. Finally, after what seemed an age, the kicks became less frantic. And then she was dead. I allowed her body to flop into the bath, resigned now to disposing of two recently deceased corpses instead of just the one I'd planned for.

I dragged both the bodies to the living room and sawed them into manageable parts, which I double and triple bagged and secured using gaffer tape. Then piece-by-piece I buried them in a variety of remote locations throughout the North. I travelled only at night and made sure that I buried the different packages in areas not frequented by the public very often.

'Ark Europa, this is your captain speaking, if I could have your attention for a moment? If you would all gaze to starboard, you will see, silhouetted now against the backdrop of Mars, Agnes, who is presently on a collision course with the Earth. For estimated time of contact, speak to your area supervisor. Agnes will remain in view to starboard for a number of days, and then will be visible from the rear of the Ark until impact. A concert will be taking place on the date of the impact to celebrate this historical date in the history of mankind.'

Braithwaite, having been the last to win a ticket, was the final scheduled to board the Ark. All Braithwaite's (My?) personal possessions had been loaded up weeks before. By the time I arrived in a taxi and pushed my way through to the boarding gate and had my retinas scanned and my prints checked, and was waved through to the waiting area, a group of protesters had assembled. They were the usual assortment of disorganized left-wingers and religious types. There was a lot of shouting, some pushing and shoving, the protesters threw some rocks which caromed off the side of the Ark's metallic carapace harmlessly, the police threw tear gas and kettled the protesters, then they battered them with riot shields and electrified truncheons. There was a lot of noise and smoke, but in the end it was all a bit anti-climactic.

The Ark was gigantic. Gigantic wasn't a big enough word. Gargantuan wasn't big enough. Colossal was probably closer. Even that wasn't quite up to it. I looked up the side of it, soaring away into the clouds. How was it, I thought, they were able to construct these sci-fi wonders? How was it that nobody from the media got wind of it? They were incredible. They were monstrous. Surely something should have picked them up, a privately owned satellite perhaps or a super long camera lens? They were staggeringly large structures. It wasn't like you could fling a tarpaulin over them to protect them against the elements.

Billionaire Investment Banker Feared Drowned

Joshua Randall the billionaire investment banker and heir to the Goldstone fortune is missing and feared dead today, following a freak boating accident off the coast of Cornwall. The Lucky Mermaid, Randall's pleasure yacht, was last seen off the coast of St Ives on Thursday. Randall was reported to have gone out in the yacht alone at 09:00 in the morning. An hour later, the Cornish Coast guard received a distress signal from Randall, though it's unclear at this point what that call was relating to. By the time the boat was discovered it had capsized. The body of Joshua Randall was not discovered. It is believed that a freak wave may have capsized the yacht and that

Randall may have been subsequently drowned. The search for Randall's body continues . . .

All through the boarding process I thought they would find me out. Even as the Ark was ascending, I was convinced I would be arrested. I remained in my quarters for some time, which were decently sized given the circumstances and well provisioned with en suite bathroom and comfortable sleeping pod. I waited for them to come for me. They never did. I waited until we were well underway before I ventured out. I found my way to the viewing deck for my level. I sat staring into the vast emptiness of space. A young lady with blonde ringlets, watery blue eyes, and skinny calves seated herself next to me. After a short while I confidently introduced myself as Gerard.

'Hello Gerard,' she said offering me her hand. 'My name is Emm—'

She checked herself and smiled briefly at her ghostly reflection in the viewing screen in front of us. 'I'm sorry,' she said. She shook her head as if to clear it. 'My name is Naomi.' She said. 'Naomi Jane Roberts! I'm incredibly pleased to make your acquaintance.'

(225-50) Agnes was first published in Perihelion Online Science Fiction Magazine (November 2015).

Jeremiah Dudd is experiencing radical biological disturbances following a skipping operation gone awry, unaware that he is the unwitting test subject in a make or break experiment conducted by the ruthless and ambitious Dr. Ignatius Welsh.

SKIPPER JEREMIAH DUDD

Jeremiah Dudd, dressed in black from head to toe, his gear—blowtorch, machete, night goggles, and crowbar—in a rucksack over his shoulder, clambered up the wall. He cut the wire and flipped himself over one handed to land deftly on the tarmac below. He rolled, ducked into the shadow cast by an HGV trailer, and waited to see if he'd alerted any guards.

The Fish had been right. Security was lax for such a big company. No cameras on this segment of wall. Nothing electrified. No motion sensors. Nothing. The only CCTV coverage was the entrance and exit to the yard. There were no guards patrolling and no dogs prowling in any part of the complex.

Surrounded by genetics texts and biological literature, Dr. Ignatius Welsh was at that moment reminiscing while reclining in a leather-upholstered chair some miles from the site of the break-in, waiting for the trial to commence in his study.

He was recalling with fondness how specimen 24, his meal ticket if things went well today, had come into being. Hard to believe now, since the preliminary trials had been completed and the secondary phase was about to commence, but Specimen 24 was conceived as a joke. It had been dreamt up in the lab by a bunch of bored genetics engineers. They were just kids really, brilliant kids albeit, some of the best minds in the country within their chosen field, but kids nonetheless, not really supervised properly, messing with invertebrates, splicing DNA sequences, mutating them, inventing strange creatures, parasites, viruses. It was only meant as a laugh, some levity between assignments. But it stopped being funny when somebody was killed.

One day the mess of DNA and ectoparasitic horror they'd fused—slime moulds, jellyfish, spiders, and scorpions—latched onto a team leader. It had already consumed his arm and was eating his face off before the room was cleared. By the time Dr. Welsh arrived with a heavily armed security delegation to destroy the mutant, (and rescue the team leader of course!) it was too late. The team leader was dead. His left arm and head were missing and half his chest had also been devoured.

That was the creature in its primal form. It had been refined somewhat since, made leaner, less aggressive. However, it was still dangerous. That was the whole point. It was an extremely potent and unpredictable specimen. Tonight's performance was to observe it in public, to observe its behavior and identify areas for improvement. There would be no more trial runs if all went well, prior to the conditioning program commencing. Production would be scheduled following this pending successful implementation of neuroprosthetic controls.

Dudd opted to search in generic waste rather than clinical. He wasn't attired for clinical waste. Clinical was often toxic anyway. If you went in unprotected, you were putting yourself at risk. His mate Denny, who used to be a quality Skipper back in the day, had once opened a clinical waste tank dressed in just his civvies. He had no protective clothing, no visor to protect his eyes. As a result, he'd ended up being splashed by something noxious. He was okay for a couple of days. Then four days after the incident, Dudd heard that the police quarantined him after he turned up rabid in the city, waving a butcher's knife and vomiting blood.

While contemplating this, Jeremiah Dudd, squatter, speed demon, and veteran Skipper extraordinaire, had managed to unlock the bins. He'd hacked the mainframe and injected it with a truth serum. It coughed up the password, no questions asked. He entered the password. He waited again, to see if there was any sort of a security response. When nothing happened he opened the bin up, sliding the electrical access door, squeezing into a gap, lighting his headset and pulling his goggles on to facilitate vision.

Memo to all Anaphylaxis Personnel:
Severe weather warning:
The company advises all staff to avoid the following areas for the next week due to severe storm and flood warnings. Please see attachment for further details . . .

The company was called Anaphylaxis Industries Incorporated. According to the local skipping contractor for illegal salvagers in the Manchester/Salford area, The Fish, security was threadbare. Also, there were a number of bins on offer comprising of clinical, chemical and generic waste. There was plenty of opportunity for the right kind of skipper.

Dudd fancied the contract. He purchased it from The Fish, a middle aged Germanic man, with gaunt features and a pince-nez clinched tightly to his beak, for thirty credits cash. He also paid the 10% finder's fee for information. For thirty-three credits he got the address, a blueprint of the yard, details of the security layout and a complementary set of wire cutters. He'd recoup his losses, he reasoned, provided that he salvaged something valuable from the bin he chose to work in.

Increase in Skipping Raids
Skipping is on the increase. As unemployment levels continue to rise and the gap between rich and poor continues to widen, more and more people are turning to skipping as a source of income. Long time

skipper and local historian Timothy R Creighton of Weaste, Salford had this to say on the subject: 'People can't afford food. They can't afford homes. They're living in the streets. Children are starving to death. There are hundreds of empty flats and houses in the area and people are squatting in them in order to stay warm. Nobody can afford the rents . . . There are no jobs . . . Crime is up. Understandably, skipping raids are increasing. These companies, the Mega Marts and corporate super hospitals and businesses and the folk up there in Cheshire with their walled in estates . . . They throw a lot of stuff away. I mean, the old saying is true; one man's rubbish is another man's treasure. Skipping has existed for years. Until you eliminate poverty you will always have skippers raiding waste dumps around the country . . .' In order to dissuade people from skipping, some food companies have been reported to be poisoning waste produce in a bid to reduce pillagers. Likewise, some of the bigger companies are investing in better security measures to put a stop to the increasingly daring and organized skipping raids that are taking place with more frequency up and down the country.

Dudd hacked his way through the trash. Finally, after ten or fifteen minutes he had a decent space to work in. He commenced the salvage operation, searching through the waste for something valuable to trade. After six hours on the job, his head buzzing from the heat and lack of air conditioning in the can, Dudd began to doubt himself. He should have kitted up. He should have gone in the clinical. You were guaranteed a payday in clinical waste, whether it was body parts to sell, organs or DNA, you always came out with something to barter.

So far the only thing he'd found in here was an old boiler. On closer inspection it wasn't even worth the credits he'd get scrapping it. There was no old tech to salvage. There wasn't any equipment from the laboratory. It was shaping into a disaster. Perhaps he should pack up and chalk it as a loss. After considering this for a moment, he packed the burner and his blade away and was just about to leave to climb the fence and bug out, when a segment of junk he'd been working at collapsed in front of him. He panicked momentarily. The thought of being buried under the refuse and suffocating to death was disconcerting, to say the least. However, a titanium case no bigger than a football thudded conveniently into his workspace. Hello-Hello, he thought. What have we got here?

Dudd grabbed at the case greedily. He exited the can. Without stopping to think, something he would have cause to regret 48 hours from now, he cracked the lid on the box with his crowbar. He prised it open gently. He placed the lid to one side. He was starting to feel excited. Maybe it was drugs past their sell by date? Somebody always wanted to buy drugs at the right price. Or blood samples from clinical trials? A synthetic kidney disposed of in the wrong place accidentally? A blast of cold air wafted up. The contents of the box smelled meaty. Dudd reached his hand in. There was something packed inside. It was cold to touch, moist and pulsing. He pulled his hand away instinctively, but he was too late, the thing in the box had bitten one of his fingers. He flung the box into the darkness, collected his bag, and then he fled from the yard vaulting the wall and stumbling away into the shadows with his bag and injured hand folded against his chest.

> *To whom it may concern.*
> *Please find attached progress report as requested.*
> *Password: Mesozoic.*
> *We have now commenced phase two of testing. Specimen 24 after a successful early trial within the laboratory has been loosed into the community for further behavioral analysis. It appears that a Skipper, a local degenerate named Jeremiah Dudd, has made contact with specimen 24. Parasitic symbiosis has*

likely been achieved. However, no further contact has been made at time of writing.

> *To whom it may concern:*
> *Please find attached progress report as requested.*
> *Password: Mesozoic 2.*
> *Further to our last correspondence earlier this evening The Skipper who was infected after tampering with the specimen box as expected, has returned to his den and is beginning to feel unwell. Surveillance is in place. Drones have been strategically deployed around the test area and are monitoring the subject's progress and movements for analysis. Subject was observed this morning picking at his arm. Information retrieved shows that antagonistic symbiosis is advancing at the expected rate. It shouldn't be long before his behavior starts to change. I'll keep you apprised of any developments as they occur. Regarding your question about how we planted the specimen, information was planted with a local skipping contractor about the flimsy security and the sizeable bins. The hope was that a local Skipper, on hearing this, would accept the contract and gain access to the refuse. Much to our excitement, the trial has gone off without a hitch so far.*

Dudd had staggered home, crashed down the hall into the living room onto the mattress feeling terrible, his temperature soaring and his stomach churning. He passed out and dreamed terrible dreams full of dead things come alive. When he awoke in the morning his temperature had come down a bit. However, he still felt wretched and so the first thing he did once consciousness returned was to check where he'd been bitten to assess what the damage was. He was appalled to find his fingers had turned black. The skin felt tough when he clenched his fist. Surprisingly, there was no pain, and when a finger came off in his hand and he accidentally dropped it into the toilet a while later, he felt strangely euphoric. He stared at the digit bobbing comically in his urine. There was still no pain. If anything he felt pleasant. As the day wore on, the infection from the bite progressed up his arm. He had to keep it covered up. When he lifted his sleeve, the sight of an oozing, sticky mess of blistering pustules greeted him. It didn't look good. He figured it was terminal. Still it wasn't hurting. Truth be told, he hadn't felt this good in years. He wrapped a bandage around it and fastened it with surgical tape. He would have to redress it regularly as the puss and slime was seeping through the gauze.

Over the next couple of days, Dudd was ravenous. He'd heard pregnant women talk about when they were craving, their appetites increased and that was how he was feeling. Only it wasn't cake he wanted, pickled products, or odd flavored ice cream, it was meat he was craving, raw and bloody. He was starting to look at things oddly like dogs and cats. It was all he could do to restrain himself from biting them. And not just animals either, he'd been looking funny at Timmy the previous night. Timmy was his flat mate, a fellow skipper and squatter. Well-known for his anti-corporate views, Timmy was a favourite with the local media who regularly interviewed him about the skipping community. They were listening to a Hendrix record using a turntable rigged to a generator. They'd cobbled the generator together using scrap metal and salvaged junk. So Timmy, dressed in shorts and a T Shirt and sporting a flat cap and beaded necklace, was like: 'What you looking at Dudd?' Dudd was like: 'I'm just thinking Timmy.' What he was thinking was, I want to rip your throat out and feast on your eyes. Thankfully Timmy wasn't aware of this. If he had been aware he'd have sprinted for the exit, bolted down the stairwell and never looked back.

Dr. Welsh, from the comfort of his study where he'd been smoking weed and sipping expensive cognac, had been making notes on his laptop for management. He'd been formulating simplistic, easily digestible emails and sending them, receiving occasional feedback and feeling smugger by the hour. The trial was a success so far.

Everyone was in agreement. There was chatter about military contracts. One response from a senior executive at Anaphylaxis mentioned how if the trial continued to be a success, bonuses and promotion opportunities would be forthcoming. Welsh placed the cognac glass on the desktop and tapped the ash out on his joint. He smiled predatorily, displaying a row of perfectly straight, bleached white teeth.

Dudd bought steaks, chicken legs, and bacon and ate them raw. None of it was enough. No sooner had he finished the last of them than he was famished and craving flesh again. He was starting to get stomach cramps. All he could think about was meat. He tried to allay the hunger by snorting amphetamine and going for a long walk. This only intensified the meat craving. He exited the flat at midnight, energized by the speed, and walked for hours, until three am before he checked the time and cursed as he was still craving meat in spite of the chemicals he'd ingested. He happened upon a timber yard in an industrial estate he'd wandered into, fenced off from the public, warning signs of guard dogs patrolling. He stepped off the path into shadow. He crouched and waited a while. After ten minutes or so, crouched in the gloom watching the yard, a Doberman slouched into view. It snapped to attention when it noted him and barked as he stepped forward. His saliva glands kicked in, he was slobbering like the animal confronting him, his stomach knotted up. His jaws had begun to work. He checked for witnesses. The street was deserted. Unable to control himself any longer, he hurdled the fence and landed on the Doberman's back and heard a cracking sound as its spine snapped. The dog jerked beneath him, kicking, howling. Dudd grabbed the dog's head. With strength he didn't know he possessed, he wrenched it hard. The dog ceased moving. Then with a great heaving yank, he pulled the dog's head off. He flung it aside. The head bounced off a stack of wooden pallets and skidded away under a tarpaulin sheet.

When Dudd returned home, despite being slathered in dog viscera from head to foot, all that Timmy could focus on was his malformed arm.

'What's wrong with your arm, Dudd?'

'Think something bit me.'

'You should get yourself checked.'

'I will if it gets worse.'

The next morning, Dudd awoke to find the infection, which had devastated his arm and pushed his appetite into the stratosphere, causing him to consume a headless Doberman in less than half an hour, had spread across his chest. It had spread down his ribcage, up his neck, across his back, down to his thigh. Fissures were appearing on his shoulder and upper torso. His blistering left arm was distorted and stretched. If he didn't know any better, and he didn't, he'd say he was growing extra limbs. Except these weren't human limbs, with hinges in the middle and hands on the end, these were alien limbs sporting mouths with fangs, boneless and slimy, incredibly flexible.

Dr. Welsh, meanwhile, continued to collate his data, arranging it into reports, sending it to management. He forgot to shave. His hair became unruly. He subsisted on a diet consisting mainly of coffee. This caused him to urinate often. His piss was smelly. It was the colour of apple juice. He was smoking constantly. His chest was starting to hurt. His eyes burned from staring at computer screens all day. He had staff to do this, younger men willing to stay up all night crunching numbers. However, he was a bit of a control freak. This meant that he had to do it himself no matter what the cost to his physical and mental state.

Management was restless, due to the infection rate slowing down. Consensus was that parasitic symbiosis should be more aggressive. The hostile takeover wasn't hostile enough. The moment when the skipper, as recorded on the footage retrieved from surveillance drones filming the timber yard, leapt over the fence like a super hero and killed the dog and pulled off its head, had happened almost a week ago. If further progress wasn't reported soon, the initial enthusiasm displayed by management would ebb away, the project would be shelved, Welsh would become a laughing stock.

Dudd was experiencing cognitive difficulties, there was no coherency to his thoughts, his speech had become jumbled and his vision was starting to go funny. He was starved constantly now and becoming more and more susceptible to violent, carnivorous urges. His ability to maintain control of himself—he'd only given in to the hunger once, when he attacked the guard dog and consumed it frenziedly the previous week—was starting to slip. The meat he'd consumed, purchased from a variety of black market stalls in the city, was no longer sufficient to satisfy his appetite. To make matters worse it was possible, no, probable in fact, that he may have killed a woman today. He'd been staggering through a local park, struggling with the increasingly confused morass that was his cognitive functioning, when a little old lady walking her dog confronted him about his health. She asked if he was all right and he shoved her away. He wasn't sure what happened next only that when he came to he was lying in an alley and it was dark. He no longer felt like Jeremiah Dudd. He was changed beyond all recognition now. Whatever ethics he'd had, whatever misguided notion of morality he'd previously clung to, had vanished into the ether never to return. He was famished and pissed off. He needed to eat something quick to sate the craving before his stomach exploded and his brain turned to slush.

> *To whom it may concern.*
> *Please find attached progress report as requested.*
> *Password: Mesozoic 15.*
> *According to reports coming in, although slightly later than anticipated, specimen 24 has finally established dominance. The Skipper is losing control. The trial is entering its final phase. Behavioral analysis is ongoing at this time. As planned, I shall be entering the fray to observe the specimen's progress shortly.*

This is to enable me, in collaboration with the information gleaned from the drones and local camera footage, to make a more comprehensive report on events as they occur. Reports will be less frequent for a number of hours. However, feel free to email me your queries and I will respond to them all as soon as I am able.

Extract from the statement of Mrs. Annabelle James regarding the murder of Mrs. Hovis and her terrier Benji.

DI Parker: So you were saying Mrs. James. About what happened in the park. One more time, please, if you could tell us what you saw.

Mrs. James: Yeah, well. I was sitting on a bench in the park, near the duck pond reading my book.

DI Parker: Go on. So where was Mrs. Hovis at this time.

Mrs. James: Walking her dog on the path by the pond.

DI Parker: And where was the man.

Mrs. James: I hadn't seen him yet. I don't know where he came from. I wasn't really looking.

DI Parker: Right. So you say you saw Mrs. Hovis walking her dog along the path. Then what happened?

Mrs. James: Well then there was this fucking great . . . I'm so sorry can you strike that out and I'll start again?

DI Parker: That's okay. Please continue.

Mrs. James: Well, he just sort of appeared, this great big thingamajig; one minute there was nobody and the next there was this man, or I think he was a man; he didn't look right not even from that distance.

DI Parker: Could you elaborate on that for us?

Mrs. James: What?

DI Parker: How did he look?

Mrs. James: It was dead weird like, he was dressed like a bloke but his clothes hung on him wrong. His face, what I could see at any rate was a right mess, all black and bleeding. The lady went up to him, God alone knows why, and put her hand on his shoulder cause he was leaned over like he was sick, and then he just exploded. He hit her with something, sort of flexible and long.

DI Parker: So let me get this right. He hit her with something, some kind of a weapon.

Mrs. James: No. It was attached to him somehow . . . anyway it thumped her out of the way, she flew across the field into the bush and then he bit the dog and he threw it into the trees. Poor dog! Picked it up like a football and fired it across the park. It flew into a sycamore tree where it was caught up in the branches and then it fell out and hit the floor and lay there dead with its legs sticking up.

The door to the squat opened and the thing formerly known as Jeremiah Dudd slid in. Dudd's flesh was slewed off. Where his arms had been, was a writhing confusion of tentacles and mandibles. Where his face had been, was a nest of poisonous fangs. He was pulsing all over. There was hair everywhere, slime and juices.

Timmy considered legging it, but was too slow off the mark. Before he could move, the creature attacked, paralyzed him with its fangs and injected digestive juices into him, rendering him into potage.

A short while later, following reports from neighbors of strange noises coming from the derelict flat upstairs, Dr. Welsh, freshly shaved, washed and dressed for his field trip in a suit and tie and black felt trilby, entered the building. He stepped around the hoarded junk, the bicycle and car parts and tools and general debris.

'Skippers,' spat the officer in charge, 'they were a right couple of hoarders and no mistake.'

Welsh smiled at the officer. He held his fake ID aloft for the idiot to observe. He ducked under the crime scene tape and into the Skipper's hideout. The place was an Aladdin's Cave of salvaged junk. It was surprisingly tidy; this in spite of the fact someone had been eaten in here recently. Various forensics folks were dotted about, puzzled expressions on their faces, trying to look as if they knew what they were dealing with. They hadn't a clue of course. This was way out of their jurisdiction. Only one of them questioned his presence. With a practiced smile he flourished his fake ID at the forensics man and confidently explained himself.

'I've been sent by the ministry for infectious diseases. I'm here to ascertain whether a panic is in order.'

The forensics man left him to it and he wandered around the room taking photographs, noting the lack of mess left by specimen 24, composing his next message in his head to management about the specimen's potential. Timothy Creighton, or what was left of him, had been totally consumed. A suited crime scene worker pointed out to the doctor that so far they'd recovered a foot and three fingers. However, there was nothing else left. Welsh took some samples for pathology. It would take these morons days to get a report back. There were some benefits to working in the private sector, Welsh considered as he swabbed the slime and bagged up his findings.

The No-Longer-Dudd-Specimen, shorn of its clothing and skin, and with no moral compass to guide it, since its higher brain function was so eroded, reverted to basic instinct. Whipping its crazy, blood spattered limbs and snapping its jaws manically the creature made a beeline for the city.

A short while later, onlookers at St Peter's square in the city were horrified to observe as the mucilaginous mess formally known as Dudd smashed through a carriage of the arriving Eccles tram. The tram, which had been trundling into the city from the direction of Salford Quays, squealed to a halt. It was obvious from the blood spatter, the rending metal sounds, the screaming coming from what was left of the carriage, that people had been injured as a result of the collision.

The creature paused momentarily, stunned perhaps from its run in with public transport. It emitted a terrifying stridulation. Then it crawled up the side of the Midland Hotel. It stopped part way up, skittered down again trailing some kind of phlegmatic discharge, and then it leapt from the building fifty feet up. Shoppers and office workers looked on, bewildered, paralyzed, terrified, transfixed by the sight of this unimaginable horror, watching with mouths agape as it hurtled through the air, airborne biological death monster from hell, plunging toward a Japanese tourist sporting a Man United shirt and pointing his Nikon skyward in a doomed attempt to capture the spectacle on film.

> *To whom it may concern.*
> *Please find attached progress report as requested.*
> *Password: Mesozoic 16.*
> *Specimen 24 has assumed full control of the host. At approximately 14:00 local time, it entered the city and engaged with the populace. The final number of casualties is not yet known. Development of the specimen however has been extraordinary. Predominantly it has manifested carnivorous invertebrate characteristics. These have proved especially formidable when navigating the urban environment. It can walk up buildings. It can jump great distances. It has displayed unnatural strength. It is able to withstand incredible force as displayed by its collision with a tram, after which the specimen sustained minimal injuries. It is incredibly quick too, which is surprising given its unwieldy physique.*
> *Regarding the flat mate, Timothy Creighton. Having myself investigated the scene, I am pleased to report that the manner in which the specimen interacted with Creighton was also a resounding success. Very little evidence remained.*
> *It is my professional opinion, given the progress we've witnessed so far, that no further trials are necessary at this juncture. All that remains is to implement the proper cerebral controls; we shall also speed up the rate at which symbiosis is achieved. A memo has been forwarded to the neuroprosthetic department for a progress report, which I will send to*

you all as soon as the report has been forwarded to my inbox.

So far the Dudd creature had killed a Japanese tourist, two old ladies out lunching in the city, a further stray dog, a solicitor on his dinner break smoking a cigarette, a vagrant begging credits next to a cash machine in Spinningfield, and a Skipper on a canal barge named Jed who was unlucky enough to be cruising down the canal in the rain when the Dudd creature was passing. Nobody had heard anything since. A number of drones had reported that Dudd had been sighted in Salford near the Quays. Surveillance had subsequently lost track of its whereabouts.

Extract from news report re: explosion in city center:

Segments of the city have been closed off today due to a reported explosion that took place near the Midland Hotel. The explosion is reported to have released a pocket of gas into the air from an underground tunnel containing rare microorganisms, sources suggest. Dr. Welsh of Anaphylaxis Industries, stated during an interview that 'Once the organism is inhaled the host becomes infected with a virus. So far the mortality rates of those infected has been 100%. The virus attacks the central nervous system, causing the victim to become violent and aggressive. Then it attacks the liver and kidneys. Approximately four hours later, multiple organ failure occurs.

Civilians are advised to stay away from the city at this time. An evacuation of the surrounding area is presently underway. The number of people killed by the explosion and subsequent outbreak of the virus, is as yet uncertain. Meanwhile residents in the immediate area surrounding the explosion have been quarantined. It has been reported that they have been removed to at an undisclosed location for further observation at this time.

Transcript of field report by Dr. I Welsh completed post trial following post trial debrief.

21:00 hours.

Operation "deep clean" commenced. Acted as 'talking head' on bogus TV interview in the city to allay suspicion and provide reassurance.

21:15

Sniffer program released online, as per trial protocol, to apprehend footage and documents pertaining to the specimen's existence. Key witnesses to the scene rounded up. Removed to a secure location for neutralization at a date yet to be agreed upon.

Continued to liaise with military and police personnel. Advised re: - 'outbreak.' Maintained story in situ re: - outbreak of unique and lethal pathogen. Continued to orchestrate fear and panic, to distract focus from trial long enough to destroy evidence and apprehend rogue specimen.

01:00

Drones have located the specimen. Specimen no longer active! Specimen reportedly gone to ground in abandoned factory, on the banks of the River Irwell, in the middle of industrial estate, surrounded by waste ground.

02:00

Extraction Team assembled. Team to extract specimen on my mark following successful engagement and subjugation of specimen.

03:00

Taxi pulled up outside target factory. Local taxi driver 'honked horn!' I suspect a bogus call from local teenagers to nearby taxi rank resulted in a cab being dispatched to this address. Noise roused specimen. Specimen agitated as a result. Distinct specimen stridulation recorded. Unable to properly observe specimen due to mediocre lighting. Able to observe outcome of specimen engagement with driver. Specimen dropped onto the taxi. Crashed out of a second floor window and squashed the taxi flat. Driver collateral damage. A drone which was too slow getting away also destroyed by creature's descent.

03:20

Order given to engage specimen. Team advancing. Specimen in retreat. Cornered specimen in factory. Three of Anaphylaxis Security Personnel lost during engagement. Sgt. James Wallace decapitated during advance. Private's John Harris and Frank Block, both disemboweled. Families notified. Specimen shot with tranquilizer darts twice before finally being overwhelmed. Specimen restrained, vitals checked and documented. Subsequently, specimen removed to laboratory (location undisclosed) for further analysis following post trial debrief.

Strange Creature rampages through City

Eyewitnesses claim a strange creature was spotted in the city today climbing buildings and attacking civilians. One onlooker who refuses to be named for fear he might be recognized, said:

'There was no gas. There were no explosions. A hole didn't just appear in the ground like magic. What I saw was a monster, some kind of biological atrocity, which smashed up the tram and killed a bunch of people.'

The Daily Lash was unable to confirm the witnesses' story though the editor did receive a further anonymous tip off stating that Anaphylaxis Industries may have been involved. A spokesperson for the company has denied the company's involvement stating that in no way shape or form did anyone affiliated with the company have any involvement with the incidents in the city.

Skipper Jeremiah Dudd was first published in Perihelion Online Science Fiction Magazine (March 2014).

When Obadiah Wickes's residence comes under attack from an unidentified assailant, revenge for a past wrong seems the only rational explanation.

A DISH BEST SERVED

The Wickes residence, which was referred to by locals as the slave-pen, due to its uncanny resemblance to a 17th century Mississippi plantation, was situated off a cobbled lane overhung by horse chestnut trees. The road leading to the house was strewn with horse chestnuts, which had fallen and been mashed amidst the leaves and churned-up mud.

There was a single entrance to the residence, via a heavily fortified gate, situated at the end of a narrow tree-lined drive and constructed of wrought iron bars topped with ornamental spikes.

A figure manned the gate dressed in polished black high boots. He wore a black woolen greatcoat and his name was Bob. Bob was a state-of-the-art security bot. He was programmed to know Kung Fu, fitted with military grade weapons systems, spoke numerous languages and made a mean cappuccino. In combination with the twelve-foot-high fence that circled the property, he was more than adequate defense against any would be intruders.

Extract from conversation with Mrs. Andrews, resident in Monton village, recounting events leading to the lynching on the green in March of last year

'So, Mrs. Andrews, you were on the road when the posse approached, prior to the incident on the green?'

'I was on Monton Road, yes, outside the shops. Been to my daughters for tea. She lives in Eccles by the library. I was on my way home when I saw them approaching.'

'Did you recognize anyone in the mob?'

'There were a few I recognized. There was Wickes at the front, the witch-finder general, waving his pistol and shouting and organizing. Then there were his lackeys trailing behind. The fat one! What's his name? Wilson I think his name is, pulling Bethia by her hair. She had her hands bound in front and her dress was ripped and bloody. Her face was bruised. One of her eyes was swollen shut. Then there was Bessie from the tower block.'

'Who is Bessie from the tower block?'

'Bessie Langford. A proper horror that one! Always going on about kicking the Extras out, petitioning for segregation in her column in her blog. There was a good few others as well, jeering and punching their fists in the air.'

'Did you see the Extra?'

'I know he was there, but I couldn't see him properly cause of the mob that surrounded him.'

'Did you see what happened?'

'No. I turned up my street after they passed so I could get home sooner. I wanted to call the police. I'm not as limber as I used to be. Took me a while to get back to the house.'

Rapid Wilson was stoned, skimming through a religious magazine, rocking backwards and forwards on a rickety porch-swing, booted feet crossed at the ankle, shotgun propped against a bucket next to the swing. He wore a nondescript baseball-cap and a print T-shirt with Otis Redding on the front.

Wilson had barely moved all evening. He would roll a joint periodically then place it behind his ear. After a while he would light it and pop lazy smoke rings the wind pulled apart.

He was supposed to be on watch. However, with Bob manning the gate and the fence ringing the building, the idea of a watchman was somewhat redundant. He'd started to nod out. The magazine slipped through his fingers. His head was starting to dip, sleep was troubling his consciousness.

A bustling wind caused the house to creak on its foundations. Trees swayed, their iron branches bending to accommodate the gale. Leaves descended red, orange, and yellowing. An owl hooted in nearby woodland. Sirens sounded in the distance somewhere.

A moment later, there was the crack of firearms, and either Bob was glitching and had shot himself in the face, or they were under attack and Bob was possibly compromised.

Extract from conversation with local deputy James Fletcher regarding the lynching on Monton Green in March of last year.

'Were you first responder to the scene?'

'I was first on the scene, yes.'

'What did you think when you arrived?'

'What a complete and utter shambles.'

'Am I right in saying, and correct me if I'm wrong, that you've previously gone on record, as have other members of law enforcement, as saying they got what they deserved?'

'It's not about what I think or whether they got what they deserved.'

'Care to elaborate that statement?'

'Fact is they broke the law. The law stipulates no man or woman of earthly origin can, nor should, engage in sexual relations with extra-terrestrials. Aside from the biological implications, the danger it poses to the female of the species, it's just not right. Humans were made for one another not beings from another planet. It's perverse. That's why the penalty for engaging in such relations is death. And it's pretty explicit, yeah, you sleep with ET you get your neck stretched.'

'So with that in mind, do you agree with members of the public engaging in such behavior?'

'What you mean is, do I agree with members of the public forming posses and lynching aliens? No, I don't agree with it. There are courts and procedures, trials and due process. However, the sentence was fitting, of that there is no doubt.'

Wilson's feet slipped off the rail. He stumbled from the swing chair, the magazine fluttered to the decking. He gripped his shotgun and stepped nervously off the porch. He moved hesitantly onto the path where he loitered with his head cocked.

Panic lit him up, setting his nerves jangling like wind chimes. Whoever had done the shooting was probably on their way here. He leveled the gun. He tried not to let his hands shake. He would be ready when they arrived and would blast them to kingdom come.

Wilson focused on the drive. Nobody appeared. This only served to magnify his anxiety. Should he check on the security bot or wait and keep a look out? He radioed Boyd in the house and informed him of what was happening. Boyd told him to sit tight. He would sound the alarm and wake the rest of the household.

Wilson scoped the woodland either side of the path. It was hard. It was too dark to see properly. He squinted into the gloom, shadows and tree branches waving menacingly.

He considered finding cover. He would crouch in the shadows observing for activity. He pondered the best position for sight lines, closer to the tree line or nearer the building? And then it didn't matter. Whoever had killed the bot and entered the gate was behind him and had him in a chokehold. He tried to stamp on his adversary's feet, to elbow him in the ribs, to kick him in the shins, but his adversary was too strong. His peripheral vision began to dim. His wrestling became feebler. His body became limp. The last thing he thought as he was going down was, fucking Extras coming here, taking our jobs and our houses and then his neck was broken and his legs kicked and his finger tightened on the shotgun trigger. He blasted his foot off as he slumped lifelessly onto the pathway.

Extract from conversation with Mr. Harris and Mr. Edwards, residents in Monton village, recounting events pertaining to the lynching on the green in March last year.

'So, Mr. Harris, you said in your statement to the police you were near the green when the mob arrived.'

'I did.'

'What did you see there that night?'

'As I said previously, I was near the green. I was walking my dog, waiting for it to shit so I could bag it and head home. I saw them approaching from Monton Road. There were a few of them, most of them I didn't recognize.'

'Mr. Edwards, did you recognize anyone in the mob?'

'I didn't recognize them either. It was much too dark. I thought I could see Wickes but it was hard to be certain. I was returning from the pub on the corner—you know the one, The Raver's Arms, opposite the church? Anyway, they strung him up. It was a proper lynching. They bound his arms, bound his feet together at the ankles, they looped the noose around his neck. His face changed colour. Must be a defensive reaction they have, like a chameleon blending with its environment. He didn't look afraid, not even when he was hoisted. Two of them secured the rope, but it was impossible to identify them from that sort of distance.'

'Mr. Harris, if I could just ask, what happened next?'

'Can I be honest with you?'

'By all means!'

'I don't know what happened next. I was worried they'd notice me so I ducked behind a hedgerow. I hid until the police appeared. Heard the shot fired, people chanting and stuff, then the cops turned up and that was the end of it.'

'Coming back to yourself, Mr. Edwards, did you witness anything more than what you've described?'

'I saw a bit of what happened. I could see the Extra hanging, kicking his multiple limbs, but I couldn't see any faces, just an alien being hung. Then I heard Bethia—I think it was Bethia—her screams echoed round the green. There was the sound of a shot fired. It was deafening and frightening. The solicitor ran up but he was much too late. Someone punched him in the face. He put his hands up to ward off blows, and then they were on him, kicking and punching, he fell to the ground and they crowded round him . . .'

William Boyd, tall, corpulent, dressed in vintage Armani and leather Gucci brogues, often menacing when dealing with the less salubrious aspects of his boss's business, was seated in his gaffer's drawing-room with the lights turned down. The TV was playing. Superhero porn flickered mutely.

The porn was wallpaper. Boyd, listening for sounds of a break-in or movement of any kind, was no longer watching. He turned a revolver in his palm, checked it was loaded, cocked the hammer and sighted across the room. He alternated his attention between the hallway and windows.

The shotgun blast, when it sounded, echoed loudly, startling Boyd from his seat. He fumbled for the radio and checked for a response. Wilson didn't answer. There was the fizz and crackle of static, wind circling the building.

Boyd telephoned for support. Communications were down. Whoever disabled Bob also jammed the electrics. Nobody could dial for help. Wi-Fi had been blocked. They didn't have a landline. They were alone here in the house.

Extract from conversation with Mr. Robert Gray, editor of the local left-wing paper The Grind.

'In terms of his political aspirations, what can you tell us about Obadiah Wickes?'

'He had no interest in politics. We can start with that.'

'So why run for office, if you have no interest in governing?'

'Being the standing MP meant he could influence policy. He could use his position to maneuver local contracts.'

'What would be the benefit of this?'

'Remember the Aliens Holding Act? Basically it was an obnoxious piece of reactive legislature. It was implemented to stop aliens, who arrived on the ship after it landed here forty years ago, from owning property. This meant any and all assets they arrived with were stripped from their possession.'

'So the government seized the ship they arrived on, once the act passed through parliament?'

'Indeed. Of course, nobody knew what to do with the interstellar equivalent of a broken-down touring bus, so the ship was sold off piecemeal to private corporations. For want of a better expression, it was filleted, the technology was sold off in the cosmic equivalent of a fire sale and the bones of it were cast aside.'

'Where did Wickes factor into this?'

'The shell of it, rising out of the Salford wasteland where it eventually came to rest like a brutalist ice-cream cone, was less coveted. Wickes saw opportunity in this brooding scrap heap. When the ship went up for auction two years ago, he put a bid in for its purchase. He'd already drawn plans up to convert it into apartments.'

'What stopped the sale going through?'

'A number of alien elders, disgusted by the notion that Wickes, who openly loathed and vilified them in the press, was bidding on their birthright to turn it into flats, contested the purchase. They hired a legal team fronted by Nightingale and Co. They drew up a counter proposal to reclaim what they perceived to be their heritage.'

'So the counter claim was holding him up? To counteract it he would enter government to influence the decision making process.'

'Exactly.

'Do you think this led to the lynching, perhaps?'

'Potentially. One can imagine Wickes finding out about the teacher's tryst with her alien lover, rubbing his hands together with glee and then doing a cartwheel for good measure. Following the cartwheel, when it dawned on him she was the niece of the solicitor supporting the Extras, he must've thought God was shining on him.'

'Why did it get out of hand, given here was this neatly packaged scandal to be exploited?'

'It didn't. The lynching, the execution of the teacher, the solicitor being informed of events and attending to save the day only to wind up in intensive care with his head bashed in, this was all a piece of well-organized theatre. It was pretty nasty theatre, it only played well to a certain type of individual, however it was effective theatre and a lot of people bought into it.

Boyd was unsure of the numbers they faced, but with swift organization, their position was defensible. There were a series of upstairs rooms, five in all, excluding the bathroom. There were three with windows that were potentially accessible and would need to be barricaded. The stairs would need defending too. Whoever was after them, sensing they were short on numbers, might try a frontal assault to infiltrate their position.

Boyd lumbered heavily up the polished wood of the staircase, muttering and cursing under his breath. The steps creaked in protest under his weight. His respirations were labored as he hurried to reach the summit.

Bessie Langford's face appeared over the bannister, the face of a lesser predator, a stoat or weasel perhaps, furtive, thin, suspicious, wan.

'Check the windows!' Boyd barked. 'Make sure they're secured. Get your derringer. You can cover the staircase. Make sure nobody comes up. If anything moves shoot it until it's dead!'

He rumbled towards Wickes' bedroom. He would check on the boss then sweep the first floor for signs of intrusion.

It occurred to Boyd as he huffed along the landing that if he'd abandoned Wickes, when it was feasible to run, after the lynching took place last year, he never would have been holed up here like this. He'd seriously contemplated leaving and not just because of the lynching either, which Wickes had gone ahead with despite Boyd's protestations. When you considered the ill-advised execution of the schoolteacher—how they were meant to recover in the polls following that was anybody's guess— not to mention the near fatal beating of the solicitor, the legal ramifications, the cost of bribing officials, the rigging of juries, the sweetening of the judge, (which caused civil unrest across the borough as activists and space-niggers, outraged at the leniency of the sentences meted out, engaged in flash protests and organized street rioting) there were plenty of reasons to abandon camp. Local opinion polls had tanked. The right-wing media, fronted by Bessie in her blog, was sluggish to react. Eventually, a meaningful counter argument was organized, but only after significant damage had been done to the Wickes campaign in the meantime.

Then suddenly the wind changed. Opinion began to favor them. Although the lynching and Wickes' subsequent denigration by the left had eaten at their popularity ratings, it was a momentary dip. The quiet conservative majority, with whom the lynching played well locally, began to rally. The polls started to improve. The lynching scandal was airbrushed out of existence.

Boyd, usually the power behind the throne, the master manipulator, able to turn a bad situation to gold, breathed a sigh of relief. He hadn't seen a way out of this. There would be no development of the crash site. There would be no meteoric rise to power. Boyd had surmised, wrongly as it turned out, it was pointless shackling himself to Wickes. The time had come for him to pack his bags. When the tide turned he was as surprised as the opposition. Clearly his boss had been right to kill the Extra. He mentally unpacked his luggage. He decided to hang around to see how it played out.

Extract from conversation with Mr. Jonathan Davidson, pastor for St Vincent's, regarding the lynching on the green.

'So you saw what happened from your window?'

'I didn't see what happened exactly. I didn't see the murders take place. I heard the commotion and went to investigate. By the time I was dressed and I'd convinced my wife to let me look, it was mostly over. Bethia, the solicitor's niece, was shot in the back of the head. She was slumped over when I reached her. I was surprised by how little blood there was.'

'What about the Extra?'

'The Extra was still hanging. His arms were dangling. Both the lower ones were twitching still. This was upsetting to observe. There was a bit of a breeze and he was turning on the rope, this way and that, swaying back and forth. We cut him down. Someone draped a coat over his face. People

took photos to document the tableaux. A group of thugs started to shout anti-Extra slogans. They soon dispersed once the police van arrived. The police cordoned off the area and took statements from onlookers. There wasn't a lot of cooperation. The crowd dispersed. Forensics turned up shortly after. We called an ambulance and they loaded the solicitor into the back of it.'

Extract from conversation with Robert Moore, author of the e-book, *Loving the Aliens.*

'I remember the day they came, almost forty years ago to the day, thundering out of the sky, trailing fire and black smoke. The news footage, the endlessly looped recordings, and the ship, a magnificent tumbling bauble, flattening buildings and devastating landscape.'

'What was the response when the Extras arrived?'

'I remember the initial response, the newspaper headlines, horror and despair at the wreckage and havoc. I remember lots of church services during this period, for loved ones who were killed following the devastating impact.'

'So opinion was negative from the start?'

'Opinion was divided. There were those who thought the Extras should be tried and imprisoned. There were those who thought it wasn't the Extra's faults, not like they were drink driving or anything, not that we know of at any rate, just that their engines failed. I mean according to reports, they never meant to come here. They were just passing through, on their way to a different system.'

'What happened next?'

'Internment camps were set up. There was head scratching from politicians. The right-wing loony contingent wanted them deported. Where to exactly none of them were able to clarify. Should the Extras remain in England? Ought they not be dispersed around the EU? They were quarantined for over a year, to make sure they weren't carrying life-threatening pathogens. They were eventually deemed to be non-contagious. Then once their internment was done, they had to be housed. They had to be fed. They had to be integrated into society. People became wary

during this period. There was less support for them than there had been previously. They were relocated around the country, cheaply housed on purpose-built estates, usually on the outskirts of cities, mostly in the north of the country. The idea was they should be segregated and policed in isolation with the minimum of fuss and minimum of cost.'

Boyd chugged from room to room, pushing past furniture using his gut as leverage, flicking window latches into place, dragging furniture to create barricades. He wasn't used to exertion of this sort. Sweat gathered between his thighs. The fat folds beneath his armpits moistened. His chest was starting to feel constricted.

At no point did he pause to consider his actions were idiotic, that the individual hunting them had penetrated the house prior to him securing the windows. It was only when a hand gripped his shoulder, spun him around and pressed him forcefully against the wall that he realized his mistake. Of course, it was too late to correct his oversight. The hand tightened its grip on his throat. He was lifted off the floor. He wondered what happened to Bessie. Why wasn't she covering the stairs like he'd asked? Then his neck was broken. He was hoisted over the balustrade and dropped like a wet rag. He landed on an antique writing bureau reduced to splinters by his blubbery mass.

Extract from conversation with Dr. Ross consultant in emergency medicine at New Salford Royal Accident and Emergency.

'Following the assault, media reports varied as to the extent of the solicitor's injuries. In your professional opinion, how exaggerated were reports?'

'I didn't observe the media coverage, but I can report that one of his legs was broken, some of his ribs were broken, he had a fractured eye socket, and his jaw had to be wired. However, those were the least of his problems. His breathing stopped when he arrived in the department. He had to be intubated and resuscitated immediately. His physical observations were erratic. He was bleeding internally. He was struggling to ventilate. We thought we

might have lost him on two further occasions at least, there was quite a bit of blood loss due to a knife wound in his abdomen. The team managed to stabilize him. He's a very lucky man. Those sorts of injuries are oftentimes fatal.'

Obadiah Wickes, seated behind a varnished teak desktop in a leather-upholstered executive chair, fiddling with the clasp on his cigar case, flicking it open and clipping it shut again nervously, considered his predicament. He'd heard the shotgun blast and observed the stricken look on Boyd's face. Then, moments after Boyd reassured him he was safe, he'd heard a crashing sound, muffled by the door. Perhaps it was furniture breaking, but it was hard to be certain from this sort of distance.

Wickes mentally ticked his colleagues off.

The expensive security guard was neutralized. Wilson was no doubt dead, unsurprising given his stupidity. Boyd was unresponsive, which was slightly more troubling. Bessie had vanished too. Most likely she was hiding somewhere. The only person left was himself. He couldn't communicate with the outside world. There was no escaping his present environment. He was cornered. The likelihood was he would be leaving here dead. Still, he was armed at least. Boyd had given him his revolver, which lay on the desk, fully loaded in front of him. He would kill anyone who came through the door. He would fire the gun at them and keep firing until the barrel clicked empty.

Further extract from conversation with Mr. Robert Gray, editor of local left-wing paper, The Grind.

'What happened after the lynching, to Wickes and his associates?'

'Wickes was arrested and a few of the others, but they couldn't make anything stick. Some say evidence was lost on purpose or misplaced by local police. Let's be honest, local law enforcement has never been very pro-active when it comes to incidents involving Extras.'

'Are you implying local law enforcement was complicit?'

'They were consciously lethargic and deliberately obtuse!

'What do you think ought to have been the punishment for those reportedly involved?'

'In a fare and decent society, they would have been found guilty on both counts of premeditated murder. Ideally, they would have suffered a similar fate to their victims, but seriously, that was never a possibility given Wickes' standing in the community.'

'So what was the closing verdict?

'Not guilty. The judge decided the evidence was inconclusive. Although there were witnesses present, none of them was able to say with absolute certainty which of the accused committed the crimes. It was a bit of a joke really. Even the solicitor didn't press charges. His memory was foggy about the beating he received. They were found guilty for breach of the peace and a couple of them served community sentences cleaning litter up and dead leaves in the city. Wickes, meanwhile, was cleared of all charges.'

Wickes touched his hair, grey close to his temples, feeling tense, his shoulders and neck aching due to stress. He was constantly getting headaches. Sometimes they lasted days. Massage didn't help. Acupuncture and painkillers proved useless.

The house was being attacked. The Extras, or somebody hired by them to exact revenge, were systematically closing in on him. Wicke's temples throbbed. Time was running out.

Wickes had killed the Extra. He placed the rope around his neck. He hoisted him into the air. Wilson and Bessie secured the rope. Wickes subsequently shot the teacher in the head. When the solicitor arrived, Wickes stabbed him in the abdomen and watched as he was beaten to within an inch of his life.

He'd conducted the lynching on the green, gambling it would increase his popularity. The expectation was that constituents afraid of Extras would be galvanized into pledging support. It would also cause damage to the

Extra's counter bid, thus killing two birds with a single stone.

He checked the revolver Boyd had given to him. He pointed it at the door-handle.

Thank God he had no family to defend, just himself, his construction business, his plans for the future. And he'd planned his future meticulously, mapping his destiny out with ruthless precision. However, that future was now jeopardized.

Following the trial, intoxicated by victory, he'd dismissed the Extras as broken and spent. Unbeknownst to Wickes, while he focused on his election campaign, the Extras were regrouping. They'd been hatching a plan and biding their time, plotting his downfall, collating their resources.

Still he had to admit, despite his present circumstances, killing the Extra and teacher, beating the solicitor to a pulpy mass, the bribes and backhanders and politics and legal costs, had all been worth it to get his hands on the ship.

His parents had died because of that ship. They were living in the city when it sucker-punched the hilltops. Their building was one of the last to be crushed, flattened like cardboard under the UFO's hull. That was why he wanted the ship, to render it neutral, to sterilize its memory by mutating it into apartments.

The door to Wickes' study burst open. Wickes fired the revolver, three times, quick succession. The weapon bucked in his hand. It hurt his wrist and rendered him deaf. His attacker, however, barely even flinched.

Wickes, dressed in kimono and velvet slippers and sporting a pair of silk undershorts embroidered with his initials, pushed his chair away from the desk, tipped over, fell awkwardly onto his shoulder, and cried out in agony. The revolver was jarred from his grasp. He attempted to crawl beneath the desk, a final refuge from the forces aligned against him, but then strong hands seized his ankles and he was dragged toward the landing. He must've hit his head on something, the door on his way out perhaps, and then he was unconscious, bouncing down the stairs, being towed from the house like a broken-down trailer.

Extract from conversation with Bessie Langford following the incident at the Wickes residence in September this year.

'So you were in the house when it was attacked?'

'I was staying in the house, yes.'

'What happened exactly, when the attack took place?'

'I was sleeping when Wilson radioed, dozing really. I'm not a big sleeper. I'd been writing a piece for my blog.'

'What were you doing at Wickes's home?

'I was his guest for the weekend, writing a puff-piece on the election and his stance on criminal Extras. Anyway, I went to look what the commotion was. I heard the shotgun go off and almost hit the ceiling. I crept to the staircase and Boyd appeared looking distraught, told me to get my gun. He told me to cover the staircase.'

'What happened next?'

'I got my gun, put my shoes on, grabbed my laptop, got my coat on and I got out of there. Out the front door and up the drive fast as my legs could carry me. I saw Wilson on the pathway outside. There was a lot of blood. I didn't investigate. I was totally panicked.'

'Did you see who was responsible for the killings?'

'Not a thing except the driveway. Then I saw the trees, then I saw the road, and then I saw a taxi and quickly flagged it down. I called the police a short while later, once the reception on my mobile had eventually returned.'

'Why did you run? If you'd stayed, you may have been able to help.'

'Let's be clear. If you think I'm hanging around to have my neck broken or head blown off by a mad alien with a vendetta, you've another think coming.'

'There was no conclusive evidence the Extras were responsible.'

'The bastards had had it in for us from the moment we left the courthouse.'

Edwin Nightingale, solicitor, socialist, pro-alien activist and middle-aged bachelor, approached the Memin with a proposal. The proposal was a simple one. He would avenge the murder of his niece and the Memin boy she'd fallen for. However, he needed help to do this. It was not an undertaking he could achieve single-handedly.

Edwin felt for the scar on his abdomen. He touched the scar on his temple where a fist split his skull, the one behind his ear where he'd been head-stomped repeatedly.

Edwin remembered everything. There was no amnesia. The forgetfulness was a smokescreen. Edwin wanted revenge. Since the legal system failed to convict, since Wickes's astonishing political resurrection catapulted him up the polls, it was inevitable he would win the election. The last thing he needed was more power. He needed to be stopped before the elections took place.

The problem was, how to go about it. Edwin, in his forties, had no training in hand-to-hand combat. He knew nothing about tactics, or how to infiltrate an enemy stronghold. He was not an athletic man. He was non-confrontational by nature. The Memin were also peaceful. However, they had a common enemy who was ruthless and dangerous.

Edwin was glad the Memin spoke English. To be able to speak Memin (which was their preferred title as opposed to the more derogatory one of Extra the media had labeled them with) required a much wider mouth and a forked tongue. Most humans, with the exception of those with body modifications, didn't possess such a muscle. It wouldn't have been useful even if they did have such an appendage. The Memin language, one-part spoken, one-part sign, was so complex, on account of them having four arms to utilize, it was impossible for humans to participate meaningfully.

After waiting for the furor to die down following the lynching, the trial, the rioting, and the media circus, Edwin requested a meet. He requested to speak with the Memin alderman whose name was Hep Memin, father of Kook Memin. Kook Memin was a car mechanic. That was how he'd met Edwin's niece. She brought her car in to be repaired. By the time she left, Kook had asked her on a date.

Neither Kook, a gentle and unassuming individual, nor Edwin's niece, a local schoolteacher beloved by her pupils and everyone who knew her, deserved to be executed. The people involved needed to be punished. The judiciary system, which failed the victims spectacularly, was no longer a viable option. The next step was *A Dish Best Served Cold.*

Hep Memin, silent, contemplative, almost holy in his stillness, reminded Edwin of a turtle, slow to move, but possessing great wisdom and authority.

'I know a guy,' he said eventually, signing unconsciously as he spoke in halting English. 'This guy... Might be... He could help. Good with AI's. You ought... To find him useful.'

Edwin did find him useful. As it turned out, Pops Memin was a childhood friend of the deceased, a software engineer, and something of a genius. Pop's specialty was AI programming. His most recent program, a security bot called Bob, was about to go into mass production.

'Why are you telling me this?'

'Prototype went missing recently.'

'By missing you mean stolen.'

'By missing I mean procured.'

'Who procured the Bob prototype?'

'Wickes procured it to boost security.'

'Does Bob have any secrets?'

'Come closer and I'll tell you.'

The Memin whispered in his ear. Edwin sputtered into his coffee mug.

'You've got to be kidding. The robot likes honey?'

'Firstly,' said the Memin, 'Memin don't kid. Second, offer Bob some honey. Offer it quickly before he blows your head off. Then the system will reboot. Honey is a back door I programmed, a joke for my brother who is an amateur beekeeper. Once system re-booted, you can upload commands. I will re-write code stream, whatever you want. I do it for my friend. You load it into system.'

'Does Wickes know any of this?'

'Nobody knows.'

'Will it definitely work?'

'Take Manuka to be sure.'

Edwin attended the Wickes residence, parked in woodland about a mile from his destination, found his way to the gate via the cobbled road leading to the drive, located the guard (who was disconcertingly dressed like an SS officer from the second world war) and greeted him like a long lost relative.

Bob demanded ID. Edwin failed to produce any. Bob threatened him with physical action if he attempted to come closer. He fired a warning shot into the ground between Ed's feet causing him to yelp in surprise and immediately retreat.

Edwin reached into his coat. He retrieved the pot of honey and offered it to the security guard. The bot holstered its pistol. It strode up to Edwin. It thanked him for his offering. It removed the pot from his hand and began to scoop the contents with its fingers into its mouth. Then it went still. A tiny drive ejected from its left temple. Edwin removed the SIM card stored inside, replacing it with a different one Pops supplied to facilitate compliance. Bob immediately rebooted. Edwin explained the plan to him. Prevent communications, kill everyone except Wickes, kidnap Wickes and bring him to the rendezvous point. Bob set off for the house. Edwin returned to the wood. He was to meet with the Memin in a clearing nearby.

An hour later Bob returned from the house. He wasn't alone however. He had brought Wickes with him, dragging him along like a length of old timber. Wickes was barely conscious as Bob lifted him into the clearing.

Edwin escorted Bob from the clearing. He would be removed from the scene and destroyed by the Memin.

Wickes got to his knees, saw the Memin appear as his eyes adjusted, evolving from the gloom, ephemeral and uncanny. There were at least twenty of them in all, gathered to bear witness, circling the accused in an ever-decreasing orbit.

Edwin placed the noose around Wickes's neck. He tightened it and handed the rope to Pops. Edwin stepped out of the circle. He watched as Wickes was hoisted into the branches. He watched his fingers twitch, spasmodic death-jerking foot-kick. Then it was done. The rope was secured. The body twisted idly in the lessening wind and Edwin and the Memin departed from the clearing.

In the distant future, a gang of salvage mercenaries attempts the perilous retrieval of a gas powered Victorian engine from the ruins of a former Northern City.

THE ENGINE

Solomon Jones was dressed in khaki, a machete strapped to his back, a bowie knife strapped to his ankle, a newly oiled Ray Gun—a custom revolver made by Raymond's of Buxton—holstered at his hip. He tied his lank grey hair out of his eyes. He shouldered his satchel with his provisions for the excursion. He turned to his team and raised his hands for quiet. The assembled persons settled down to listen.

'I'll start with myself then go clockwise around the room. Please give your name and briefly explain what your role is. Tell us your favorite colour and what your favorite weapon is, then anything else you can think of that might be interesting. I'll start with myself. My name's Solomon, I'm team leader. I'm the brain of the operation. My favourite colour is red. My favourite toy is this gun at my hip. So, who's next?'

Ellroy leaned forward with his hands on his knees. A muscular man in his mid-thirties, he had an enviable tan from his years in the sun, a waxed moustache that curled at the edges, muscular arms, and flintlock eyes.

'I'm Ellroy,' he growled. 'I'm second in command. If you have any queries about things, any concerns you'd like to discuss before we set out, come and see me after the briefing. Oh, and my favorite color is purple. My weapon of choice is chopper here.' Ellroy lovingly tapped the tomahawk on his belt.

Up next was Simpson, a twenty-year-old mercenary from Yorkshire, with a penchant for wearing homemade papier-mâché masks to hide the extensive facial scarring she'd received during a knife fight with a former lover. She was a crack-shot riflewoman whose favorite colour was burgundy. Prior to hiring her, Sol had expressed his concerns about her aim, given her unconventional headgear. To allay his fears, in a shooting exhibition she had fired three bullets from three hundred yards in rapid succession. Each bullet hit the bulls-eye dead center. Sol was impressed. Hiring her was a no-brainer.

Finally, there was Glock. Glock, with his cannon ball head and tribal tattoos, his modified bulk and humorless grin. The molded plastic of the chair buckled beneath him. His hands were big as plates and his legs thick as colonnades.

Glock's task was to carry the engine. He was also on board to help carry provisions. Glock had difficulty articulating due to damage done to his vocal chords, caused by muscle enhancers, implants, boosters, and upgrades he'd installed, not to mention the maintenance work he'd had done, some of it on the cheap, to remain a colossus and a viable mercenary.

'So where's the guide?' asked Simpson.

'He'll join us in the morning. His name is Goff and he's highly recommended.'

Three days earlier, in the trade town of Sintelins, Sol had been in The Rocket attempting to get smashed. With no job offers to speak of and his finances dwindling, both he and Ellroy were considering contract killings. Last orders had rung. Sol had finished his ale and bid goodnight to Ellroy. Stumbling from the pub, he tilted through the doors, decidedly uncoordinated due to the brew he'd consumed. A pair of hands shoved him into the street. The rain did little to sober him. Disorientated by booze, he lumbered into a doorway and slumped against the brickwork with his jacket over his head.

When he came to, he was seated in a large room. Bespoke furnishings surrounded him. A pianoforte stood in the corner of the room. A bookshelf crammed with leather bound volumes jutted behind it.

Solomon was seated in a reclining chair. He was wrapped in a kimono that smelled of orange blossom. The chair was angled in front of a roaring fireplace that was big as a cave mouth and piled with logs. Above the fireplace was the head of a taxidermied bear mounted on a plinth with its jaws gaping menacingly.

'I have to say I'm slightly disappointed. You were highly recommended by a mutual associate.'

Bilious Smart, local businessman and town leader, corpulent, red faced, tuxedoed and perfumed, materialized from the shadows. He extended a pink hand to shake. Solomon clasped it and shook it cautiously.

'Care for a drink?'

Solomon accepted a whiskey.

'Correct me if I'm wrong, but have you not been languishing in the town of late awaiting a project?'

Sol nodded.

'Is it safe to say that if a project presented itself you would be interested in a discussion.'

'Pretty safe.'

'How long would you need to assemble a team?'

'Depends on the project. If it's a big project it'll take a while. If it's smaller, if it's nearby, if the payment is appropriate and resources available, not so long.'

Bilious tipped into the chair opposite. 'It has come to our attention there is an engine in the city.'

'There's plenty of engines but most of them are useless.'

'This one isn't.' Bilious leaned forward. He whispered conspiratorially.

'It's a Victorian. It's a Crossley. Gas powered. Rare. Compact, well preserved, reasonably easy to transport.'

Solomon smiled. 'So tell me . . . how much would you be willing to pay for this Crossley, provided I can retrieve it and return it in one piece?'

Bilious clapped his hands together. He poured another whiskey. He offered it to Solomon. Solomon waved the glass away.

They met outside The Rocket. They dawdled waiting for the guide to show. Eventually, a skinny individual wearing thick frame glasses, walking boots, a waterproof jacket, and baggy shorts emerged from one of the hotels opposite. He was bowed under the weight of his rucksack. He spotted them and raised his hand. Nobody returned the greeting. After a moment's consideration, he ambled over.

Goff introduced himself tentatively.

Simpson grunted by way of acknowledgment.

'Bout time.' said Ellroy.

'Let's go!' said Sol.

Glock placed his hand on the guide's rucksack and removed it from his back. He clipped it to his belt buckle and pushed him into the road.

The first part of the journey was uneventful. They discovered a body hung from a sycamore branch as they wended their way through the ghost town of Warrington, it's lower jaw was missing and its shoes were also gone. Its trouser legs flapped raggedly in the breeze. They encountered another corpse outside Tyldesley, this one flyblown and bloated, its hands bound, its head missing where it had been severed at the neck. They encountered some carnivorous oddities, mutated descendants of the biological test subjects from the glory days of Anaphylaxis Incorporated, human-animal hybrids with strange appetites. The creatures were visible from the road, multiple limbs wafting around, busily stripping the carcasses of anonymous quadrupeds.

They reached the trading post of Boothstown on the outskirts of Salford. The post was abandoned, the gates to the town hung from their hinges. All that remained were crumbling brick terraces. The wind howled through broken makeshift windows. Ghosts drifted forlornly amongst the debris.

Solomon held his hand out. A riflescope was slapped into it. Sol wiped the lens. He scanned the road ahead, the broken, uneven tarmac, the ramshackle old homes, smoke rising from the occasional functioning chimney, the rusted bones of vehicles, the trees and bushes grown wild and unchecked.

They continued toward the city. They stayed away from waterways and rivers where the bigger creatures idled. They killed a beast they found injured by the roadside, clearly another descendant of genetic modification, some sort of bovine monstrosity, which from a distance seemed harmless, but up close was rabid. The animal rounded on them as they approached, and its gentle features split open to reveal a mouthful of razors and a lashing tongue. Solomon shifted peripherally. He crept behind it through the foliage and shadows. He cut its throat open in a single, fluid movement. The creature thrashed. Blood washed the moss-carpeted tarmac.

They moved through parkland grown wild, housing turned to rubble, roads turned to woodland and oak-fern and nettles. The woodland cleared eventually. Manchester's skyline loomed.

'Ladies and gentlemen, I give you civilization. Time to load your weapons. Keep your eyes peeled for snipers. Watch for anything that might resemble the cow we met earlier, creatures of dubious character, that sort of thing. Look out for booby traps because the city is riddled. Also, try to enjoy yourselves out there. It can be quite stressful, people shooting at you, monsters trying to kill you, friendly fire, your leg stuck in a mantrap. The thing is to enjoy it. Take pleasure from your work. Take pleasure from your work and that's half the battle.'

Solomon nodded to the guide who stepped forward.

'Not far off now,' Goff explained. 'See that old building up ahead, with the trees on the top?'

Solomon knew the building, the old Hilton Hotel, once visible for miles around it had dominated the skyline. Now the top half was collapsed. All that remained was a fire-ravaged stump, broken and ruined, crowned with vegetation.

'That's where we're going. According to Sol's intelligence the engine is nearby. There was once a museum in the area, Castlefield on the map. According to the planner, we should arrive there in an hour.'

They moved cautiously into the city, making minimal progress. Fear of traps slowed advancement. Trip wires had to be negotiated, covered pits lined with razor wire, animal dens and nests, waterways and rubble. What should have taken an hour took the best part of a day.

Thankfully, while the guide considered a route and they fretfully negotiated it, they were not attacked or set upon by monsters.

They crossed the river, traversing the bow-arched bridge on Irwell St, which was the safest point according to the guide. They inched across, taking care to avoid obstructions. The river was sluggish below. The sky sagged over them, lead-colored and miserable.

Sol cursed the weather and the bloated belly of the sky and the constant threat of rain and the foul smelling river. He cursed the guide ahead of him. He hated guides. He hated that they were specialized, which made them all uppity. They were expensive too. They were occasionally dishonest. They always believed they should get a substantive cut of the spoils. They were useless in a fight. They were more likely to hide in a corner than pick up a gun.

Sol remained behind Goff, scanning the environment for potential dangers. Goff was up ahead with his maps and compass out. He stopped suddenly. He dropped his compass. His papers scattered. They fluttered to the ground. His hands scrabbled at his throat where the shaft of a crossbow bolt protruded from his neck just above his clavicle, embedded in his trachea. He gurgled momentarily, blood gushing over his hands and lips. He stumbled onto his knees, then slumped over like he was praying.

'Take cover!' Sol shouted. The team members went to ground.

A further volley of bolts and arrows whistled around them. Solomon crouched behind a crumbling wall. Ellroy sought cover behind a blackened tree stump with Simpson crouched beside him. They waited as a further barrage of missiles rained down. They watched as an arrow pierced the shoulder of the guide flopping him over so he was staring right at them.

Solomon unholstered his ray gun, scanned for enemies, waited. There was a building across the street, possibly an old hotel, with trees growing in the guts of it, nothing to indicate movement. Solomon wavered. There was a flash of colour, the thud of a crossbow bolt as it buried itself in the ground, the sound of glass breaking, a shot fired from Simpson's rifle, somebody shouting in one of the buildings.

'Where's Glock?' Asked Ellroy.

'Over there!' Sol answered. 'He's looking upset, which might be a good thing.'

As if to illustrate how upset he was, Glock dropped what he was carrying, stood up and ran off, charging in the direction of their attackers. He was incredibly limber for such a brute, stepping to avoid arrows, ducking, rolling to avoid projectiles. He hurdled a pile of scrap, bounded a rusted car bonnet, and then he was gone, crashing into an overgrown hedge, vanishing from sight into rampant vegetation.

There was a moment of stillness. Birds tweeted in the trees. Somebody screamed. A human body emerged from the foliage. It travelled a considerable distance and struck a wall with a sickening smack.

'Gang member?' said Sol.

'Possibly.' said Ellroy.

'Possibly a rival?'

'Difficult to say,' said Ellroy.

Another scream followed the first; a ripping sound like material being torn.

'They've stopped firing at least,' Sol said.

Simpson gave him the thumbs up.

'Must've scared them off,' said Ellroy

'Not really surprised,' said Sol. He got to his feet. He dusted his pants methodically.

Ellroy stood up. Simpson adjusted her mask.

'Think your man's shoes will fit?' said Ellroy

'The guide's or the other's?' said Sol.

'Thinking of the guide's.'

'I reckon they're too small.'

'So where to now?' asked Simpson.

'We look for the museum. It can't be far off since we're nearly at the Hilton.'

Just then, Glock exited the foliage dragging a man by his ankle. The man was bloodied, semi-conscious and groaning.

'Change of plan,' Sol exclaimed. 'Let's ask your man for directions.' And he rolled up his trouser leg and unstrapped the bowie knife.

After breaking the man's arm and pressing the knife into his left bicep, Solomon learned that Pie Face, the scrawny individual wearing corroded body armor held together with twine, didn't want to die. He also learned that the attack had been an ambush, the ambush consisted of six men left behind on the orders of Bellamy.

Bellamy was in charge of the team. He was an all-round murderous bastard. Bellamy was ahead of them. He'd located and moved the engine already. He'd observed them infiltrating the city and set up this ambush with the intention of extermination.

'Who's Bellamy?' asked Simpson.

'A rival,' said Sol.

'He's a bastard,' said Ellroy.

'And he's crafty,' said Sol.

Solomon's last encounter with Bellamy—but by no means his first—occurred over a year ago on the outskirts of Hull and ended in disaster. A member of Sol's team (the guide, if memory served correctly) had double-crossed Sol, resulting in the rest of the team being massacred. They were ambushed on the return leg of their mission. Sol and Ellroy escaped by the skin of their teeth, but not before they'd abandoned the painting they'd been commissioned to retrieve, in an effort to buy some time and facilitate their departure.

Sol considered their predicament. If Bellamy knew about the engine, then others would also know. Maybe they hadn't arrived yet. Maybe they were watching, waiting for a chance to strike. This could end up ugly. Fatalities had already been recorded.

'Round up the bodies,' Sol ordered. 'We don't have much time. Put your man's arm in a sling. He's going to help us to find that engine.'

Sol organized a brainstorming session. He drew some diagrams in the dirt, using a stick snapped off a birch sapling, and a ruse was devised. They would pose as Bellamy's men, dressed in the dead men's clothes. They would rendezvous with Bellamy, then kill him and take the engine.

'Now I agree with Simpson,' said Sol, after she'd voiced her concerns. 'Dressing in your enemy's clothes, in order to pull a fast one on him, sounds a bit clichéd. Still, the best plans, the ones that tend to work and not end up a smoldering ruin with everyone a corpse, tend to be the simple ones. Plus, we have employee of the month here acting as herald. If anyone hails us, Pie Face can respond. For the benefit of Pie Face—I know you're listening tit head—if he fucks us over I'll shoot him in the head. So, to go over it one more time then, we advance on the rendezvous point at the Victoria Warehouse in Old Trafford. Once we get close enough we open fire. There are only six of them left. Surprise is our ally. Also, we have Glock. While Bellamy is watching us, Glock will outflank them. He'll attack from the rear and put paid to any stragglers. So? Anyone have any questions?'

'I have a question,' mumbled Simpson through her facemask. 'Is there any chance we can break for some lunch?'

'Take a ten-minute break. Have something to eat, make sure you go to the toilet, have a smoke if you fancy. Then we'll be setting off. Any more questions?'

There were no more questions.

'Good, we'll reconvene here in ten minutes.'

They travelled out of the city, adjacent to the canal, a damn sight faster with Pie Face leading the way. Before they knew it, they'd arrived at their destination. They parted ways with Glock, who despite his bulk, melded with the shadows and melted into the undergrowth.

They advanced toward the warehouse. The Victoria warehouse building was a ruin. Behind it, rising out of the tangle of roots and weeds like a wounded animal, was the Old Trafford football ground. Not much of it was visible yet, only the front of the ground. You could imagine it in days of yore, when it was intact and glorious and successfully lit up. Now it was dirty. It was covered in brambles. All the windows had been put out. Parts of the front of the structure had collapsed. There was nothing to indicate the building's splendid history. The only reason Sol knew of it was that he'd seen it in old photos in public houses he'd lodged in.

As they neared the warehouse, Sol couldn't see anybody. He was beginning to think that Bellamy had moved on. They were a hundred yards from the building, covering the ground rapidly. Suddenly, a figure emerged from the rubble.

'Who's that?' asked Simpson.

'Bellamy,' said Sol.

'And how would you know?'

'He's shaped like a beer keg.'

Bellamy was dressed in a boiler suit and boots and wearing a (pig?) mask to appear sinister. He raised a hand to halt their advance. He shouted for the password. Simpson looked to Pie Face.

Pie Face looked puzzled. 'What the fuck is he on about? There isn't any password!'

Bellamy laughed. He ducked out of view for a moment and Sol began to wonder. He returned carrying a rifle. He raised it to his shoulder, aimed, and fired. The shot rang out like church bells on Sunday.

Solomon stood transfixed as Pie-Face's head exploded. The bullet hit him in the jaw. It deflected into his cranium. The top of his head was blown off in a geyser of scrambled brains. Sol lurched for cover. A bullet ricocheted off a nearby rock. Ellroy was flat on the ground behind a dirt bank not far off. Solomon checked for Simpson. Initially he missed her in the dust thrown up by the scramble for cover. Then he spotted her ahead of them, near to the tree line bordering the canal, stumbling about, groaning like a drunkard, her hands holding her guts in, blood pooling at her feet. Simpson stepped forward then to the side a couple of paces, she was clearly disoriented as a result of her injury, then the ground gave out beneath her and she vanished into the hollow. She yelled in surprise but immediately went quiet.

Solomon lay still. He kept his head down. He gestured to Ellroy.

'How bad is it you reckon?'

'Pretty bad given our position! I reckon we're pinned down. Sitting ducks, so to speak.'

'Any sign of Glock?'

'No sign of him yet.'

'I wonder where he got to.'

'Probably got killed. So what's the contingency, presuming he's dead, and given their advantage up there in the warehouse?'

'Pray for a miracle. Plan for withdrawal.'

'Then you best get planning or we'll likely be fodder.'

Sol was considering an exit strategy when he spotted something in the canal. He gestured at Ellroy, nodding toward the water.

'What's that?'

Ellroy looked puzzled.

'Any idea?' he asked.

'None whatsoever! Still, judging from the direction it's headed I'd say Bellamy could be in trouble. Estimated time of arrival, next five minutes.'

Solomon held his breath as yet another hybrid, a malformed, lamprey-headed, amphibious enormity, emerged stealthily from the murky brown water. It paused momentarily and angled its head. Then it surged up the banking and vanished into the greenery.

Inevitably a few minutes later, they heard shots fired, injured animal sounds, men screaming—which is not the most reassuring noise ever—a wet sort of sucking sound that was phlegmatic and sticky, finally a percussive explosion that echoed into silence.

'Give it a few beats, and we'll go and have a look. We best take it slow though to avoid any traps.'

Simpson was dead. That much was clear. She'd fallen into a pit that was lined with sharpened sticks. Solomon glanced down at the mess in the hole, then retrieved the girl's rifle and handed it to Ellroy.

Ascension was slow and uneventful. Eventually, after a period of scrambling, over tarmac, rubble, glass, and old wire, they alighted on the warehouse. Bellamy's campsite was located inside. There was a canvass tent and a cooking fire reduced to embers. There was evidence of a fight too, plenty of blood-spatter, the cordite smell of firearms, drag marks leading to bushes.

Bellamy's men, Sol counted five of them strewn around the campsite, had been completely decimated by the rampaging hybrid. Four of them had been mauled. One of them had lost his legs and bled out. A further two had been decapitated. The forth had a hole in his chest you could fit a clenched fist in.

Finally, the fifth member of the team was slumped against a wall. He had a grievous neck wound but was not quite dead. Ellroy took pity on him. He gave him some water from his canteen. He stroked his head briefly while he sipped and gurgled. Then he retrieved the tomahawk from his belt. He split his head open, thus ending his suffering.

After a period investigating, Sol discovered a number of rifles, crossbows, shell casings, and a grenade launcher which had been fired and discarded to the rear of the site. This accounted for the explosion they'd heard earlier. There was no sign of Bellamy however. They presumed he'd been savaged and made off with by the monster. Sol scanned about for his nemesis. He discovered the pig-mask Bellamy had been wearing. It was split down the middle and spattered with ooze.

The engine was intact, set away from the action, covered with a tarpaulin and undamaged by the conflict. Sol considered how to move it.

Thankfully Glock, with Bellamy flung over his shoulder like a rolled up carpet, strolled casually into the campsite and deposited Bellamy on the floor. Solomon approached Bellamy's prostrate form and kicked him once hard in the ribs.

'Get up!' said Sol.

Bellamy wobbled to his feet. He raised his hands up, thrusting his palms out defensively. He was covered in dirt and blood, but there were no obvious signs of injury.

'You kill the hybrid?' asked Sol.

'I think I might have hurt it.'

'You shoot it with the grenade?'

'I shot it and hit it.'

Solomon considered this. He studied Bellamy who, begrimed and quivering, was totally defeated.

'How about we discuss this?' Bellamy asked nervously.

'What's to discuss?' Sol said. 'Shall we start with how you plotted to kill my team again, how you've robbed me of at least three artifacts in the last four years, how if I let you go, I'll no doubt regret it? No thanks,' said Sol. 'I'm finished with discussion.'

Sol pointed Simpson's rifle at Bellamy, who smiled and shrugged. Bellamy raised an eyebrow, mocking and inflammatory. Solomon shot him in the chest. The impacting bullet wrenched him off his feet. He was blown backward—catastrophic gut punch. He hit a wall like a wet cloth. He slid to a sitting position, head lolling sideways, jaw unhinged. His tongue flopped out. Solomon placed the rifle on the ground. He sauntered over and patted down the corpse. He removed a silver case of hand rolled cigarettes. There was also a dagger with a silver hilt. Finally, there was a pocket-sized bible, which he thumbed briefly before stuffing it into his trousers.

'So what's next then?' Ellroy asked. He was massaging wax into his moustache and twisting and curling it with his thumb and forefinger.

Sol tossed one of the cigarettes to him. He sparked it up using embers from the fire.

'Smoke that. Help Glock rig the engine up. Check the bodies, search for provisions.'

'And then?' asked Ellroy.

'Then payday!' said Sol and he leaned against the engine and chuckled and smiled.

Following the arrest for murder, trial, and subsequent execution live on television, of his brother Archie, private investigator Brady Harris receives an email that calls into question the veracity of the verdict.

VERDICT

I keep a low profile following my brother's arrest. When the photographers and media persons hide outside my flat, taking photographs, accosting me about my childhood, I decide to take a holiday where none of them will find me.

I don't know if he's guilty. We hadn't been in touch recently. He might not be a murderer, but there's no way I can help him. There's no way to contact him now that he's in custody. Nobody is allowed access once the defendant has been arrested.

I book into a guesthouse, anonymous Lake District nondescript peripheral. I work a missing person case, drink coffee, and eat breakfast. I explore the hilly paths and avoid watching The Verdict. I shower twice a day and circumvent public places.

In spite of my efforts, it's hard to avoid completely. There's a screen in the guesthouse foyer tuned permanently to the coverage. On occasion, when my attention wanders, away from my coffee and the job that I'm working on, I find myself drawn to the events on-screen. Like any bad television experience, it's impossible not to watch.

The trial lasts three days. Day one and two are dedicated to the prosecution. The evidence against my brother is presented to the public. Archie remains seated in a glass box with his head bowed. He appears to be sedated for the duration of the trial, unable to participate in his own defense, his hair is greasy and he's wearing a cheap suit procured for him by The Network. His hands are bound in front of him with flimsy looking plasti-cuffs. During summarizing, he glances up. However, it is a brief moment of comprehension after which he immediately slumps into a drug induced stupor.

Subsequent to the prosecution's summary there is a four-hour delay. During this time the public casts their votes. They call The Network and choose from either option a (Guilty), or option b (Not Guilty). Once the lines close and the votes have been counted the verdict is read out on air. My brother is judged to be guilty on four counts of first-degree murder. This is a unanimous decision the sentence for which is hanging by the neck until dead. After a moments pause, during which my brother's sole response to being sentenced to death live on air is to drool onto his necktie like an end stage dementia patient, he is removed from the dock. He is led from the courtroom with his feet dragging behind. Two burly men push a side door of the court open. My brother vanishes out of sight into custody to await his end at the hands of the media.

The third day kicks off with a brief word from the show's host, Jeremy Jupiter, who moves around the studio like a snake, asking audience members how they voted. Following this the show cuts to a ten-minute montage of the killer's exploits, complete with dodgy perpetrator pictures and sensationalist biography. This is followed by a short piece involving the arresting officer, who patronizingly explains to the viewing public how my brother was apprehended. Then there's a profile of my brother's victims with particular attention paid to the last victim, Hungarian immigrant Katalina Berenyi. Finally, the camera pulls back to reveal a backlit gallows on top of which is the kneeling silhouette of my brother with a noose around his neck, awaiting execution.

The show cuts to Jupiter in the studio looking serious. He is holding a comedy microphone with a foam head attached.

'Ladies and gentlemen the lines are now closed, your votes have been counted, the sentence has been passed.

Archie Harris, the man responsible for these heinous crimes against women—The Salford Strangler as our friends in the media have dubbed him—is to be killed by hanging live on air. But first, a word from our sponsors over at Somy. And don't forget, you can watch the highlights from this month's series of The Verdict in an hour long special on Monday after the football . . .'

According to the statistics, pedophiles being 'tried' on air and summarily executed achieve the best ratings. A good serial killer on the show also guarantees a ratings boost. Other criminals that cause a ratings upsurge are sex killers, celebrity murders, criminals with learning disabilities (due to the ethical conundrum this poses and the inevitable controversy that ensues.) and crimes of passion.

The camera pulls back slowly to reveal my brother's unshaven face. He is blindfolded. His lips are cracked from dehydration. He is saying please, please, please over and over again. He's sobbing intermittently. There is a noose tied around his neck. He is kneeling down. His hands remain tied in front of him. There is a couple of seconds' interval, during which the music builds to a dramatic crescendo. There is a cut away to Jeremy Jupiter solemnly idling in the studio. Then the verdict flashes up at the bottom of the screen, guilty by unanimous decision. The trapdoor opens and my brother is dropped.

I return home two days after the show airs. The media swarm has thankfully dispersed. The body is returned to me following the hanging. I hastily arrange for a cremation to take place. I want to avoid further media attention. The last thing I need is a prolongation of Archie's infamy. I receive his ashes in an urn. I take them to where we lived as children, the area we grew up in the city. I spread them over the rugby field we played in as kids. Subsequently, I return home. I check my emails, something I've not done for a while, I'm sifting through them looking for a mail I'm expecting regarding the case I've been working on. And that's when I notice, an anonymous mail from an unknown address, I must have missed it the last time I checked. It pre-dates the trial by a number of days. I open the mail up. The message is brief. I scroll through the contents. I read and re-read them.

'I need to speak to you about something, Pip. When you get this message skype me. It's big. You're the only person I can trust with the information.'

Only my brother ever called me Pip. It's a reference to Great Expectations. I would read it to him when we were kids, under the covers, after the lights were out. What did he want with me, I wonder? Did he want to confess? Is there another reason he mailed me? This information he mentions, was it related to his work?

My suspicions begin to percolate. I decide to do a bit of digging. I'll ask around, check out some sources, see what I unearth, the least I can do.

I research the victims on line. I search for photographs, articles, reports, and statements. Little is known of the first three victims. Two of the girls were transients. The authorities were unable to identify them. The third was a sex worker named Brandy Wine. Nobody knew what her real name was. Her narrative was mysterious. Historical details were contradictory at best. There was no next of kin identified, she had no friends in the area, her neighbors barely spoke to her and her coworkers even less so. The police assumed one of her client's murdered her. Two of her regulars were arrested in connection with the killing. Statements were taken from them both. Their alibis checked out. They were subsequently released. There were no further charges.

The final victim, Katalina Berenyi, was a 20-year-old Hungarian immigrant. She worked as a seamstress in a Salford factory. She had a cousin who lived locally. They went out drinking together at weekends. Witnesses were able to identify her. A bartender remembered my brother's face. This was on the night of her murder. He remembered Katalina. He identified them both from photographs. He described my brother as irritable. Katalina, meanwhile, was distressed about something. She was very pretty he said. She was wearing a cut off denim jacket and flower print dress for the warm weather.

I ask to see the evidence. I ask for the arrest report, which mysteriously vanishes. I ask for the video footage to be gone over. I ask to make sure it hasn't been doctored. Nobody will assist me. I ask to see the murder weapon, which nobody will allow me access to, to the DNA report that supposedly links my brother to at least three of the strangler's crime scenes. I try to get access to my brother's flat. I am initially denied access. By the time I get access it's been re-plastered and painted. A new kitchen has been installed. A fresh carpet has been laid. I continue to press the authorities. Eventually my tenacity is rewarded with an attempt on my life, which at least confirms that I was asking the right questions.

I visit the bar where, according to reports, my brother was identified with the seamstress from Hungary. I question the bartender who fingered him. I show him a photograph of my brother. He flinches ever so slightly. He lies about remembering him. There's something off about his statement.

I visit my brother's workplace next, ask for the editor, edge my way through the run down second story trash magazine offices of 'Goo' with its poor lighting, noisy dialogue, stale air, and stressed hacks. I wait in an office, stuffed to bursting with files and old Goo magazines. He eventually turns up, middle aged and breathing heavy, apologizing profusely and slopping coffee from two grimy mugs.

'I just want to know,' I ask leaning forward on my elbows. 'What was Archie working on before he was picked up?' I sip at the plastic tasting coffee that's lukewarm from the coffee machine. I place it on the editor's desk, resolving never to drink from it again.

'I'm not sure,' his former boss says. 'Men claiming to be from the police entered his office. They removed his laptop with his files and belongings. The next we heard he was on the news being arrested.'

After speaking to the editor, which didn't yield much by way of new information, I speak to some of the journalists and paparazzi milling around. I find out from the woman who shared his office, Stacey Monroe is her name, flirty young thing who fits the stereotype of a gossip columnist perfectly, that he mentioned to her in passing, shortly before his arrest, that he was working on a profile of a well-known TV host. He wouldn't divulge which program he meant. It was pretty obvious that the host was Jeremy Jupiter. As far as Stacey was concerned that was the last thing he worked on prior to his arrest.

I return home, following a brief diversion to the local curry house. I arrive to find my flat has been ransacked. I'm quite minimalist. Nothing much has been damaged. Still, I feel angry. I feel violated. I realize that if I intend to continue my enquiries I will have to make provision for escalating hostilities.

Reports indicate that Katalina, along with the other three victims, was sedated and raped. Following being violated they were strangled to death using a computer cable. The bodies were then wrapped in muslin, head to toe like mummies. They were displayed in public, exhibited like civic artworks.

In the run up to my brother's execution, an elaborate rationale was given for this. The killings were the work of a serial killer obsessed with ancient death rituals, etc. However, to my mind my brother had no knowledge of such things. This meant that he potentially wasn't responsible and somebody else had perpetrated the killings.

After the authorities had stonewalled me, but prior to the attempt on my life, I return to speak to the bartender. I want to know what he saw the night of the murder. I wait until he's closing. I enter the bar for the second time in a week.

'We're closing,' says the bartender and continues to polish glasses.

'Not yet,' I inform him and I pull up a stool. 'I need to ask some questions if you can spare me a minute.' I place a twenty on the bar to retain his attention.

'I already told you what I know.'

I place a ten on top of the twenty. He continues to polish the glass. So I offer him my watch, an expensive trinket that was a gift from a client who'd tasked me to find his missing wife.

'I could get killed for talking to you. Who's to say the men who spoke to me aren't watching us right now? They have technology these men. They have ways they can listen to people.' The barman turns the watch over. He's attempting to judge its authenticity. He's trying to figure whether it's worth taking the risk.

'Nobody followed me here, I'm positive about that. Nobody could have identified me when I came through the doors. I had my hood up, like this, so there weren't any witnesses, just you and me and the eye in the sky there.' I point to the wall-mounted camera scanning the bar. The barman shrugs in acknowledgement of the camera.

'You can never be too careful.'

'I completely agree. That being said, my advice would be to hand over the camera footage before I leave. That way, there's nothing to link you to me once I exit the premises.'

The landlord places the watch behind the counter out of sight. Reluctantly, he begins to talk. He tells me how two men paid him a visit. They were blonde, tall, wearing trench coats, packing shotguns. They told him what to say. They made him repeat it. He lost his temper and they threatened to murder his family.

'I'm sorry,' he says. 'But I love my girls. I was scared out of my wits. They were serious looking men.' Following the visit, he'd had the camera installed over the bar. 'For evidence,' he says, 'in case they come in again.'

'Go get me the footage,' I tell him. He disappears into a back room and returns holding a peg. I take the peg off him. I thank him for his honesty. I leave the way I came in, taking care as I go to check nobody is waiting for me as I exit.

Inevitably, a few days later my front door is kicked in. A couple of gentlemen in trench coats with square haircuts and serious faces, carrying pistols with suppressors attached, push into the room. They move silently around the flat. They check each of the rooms individually. Eventually one of them notices the laptop, which I've left open for them on the kitchen worktop. I wave at them out of the screen. I am seated on a bar stool across the street, sipping pale ale in The Sinking Lifeboat, busy eating lunch. I point to the timer in the bottom left of the screen. This was activated when they entered. I mouth an apology. Then the bomb is triggered. The screen immediately goes fuzzy. The windows of the pub are blown in. Car alarms up and down the street begin sounding. The bomb I've rigged takes out most of the third floor of the building opposite. I finish my drink as people run around and point and take photos of the flaming debris. I leave a tip on the bar as I exit, and make my way quickly down the street.

So the facts as I now know them are as follows:
Fact 1:
The evidence against my brother is circumstantial. However, through its use of sensationalism and misdirection, The Network, possibly in collaboration with elements of the police force and government, has managed to orchestrate his public execution.
Fact 2:
Serious men have been sent out to kill me for asking about it.
Fact 3:
I have to expose some of the men responsible for this if I am to stand any chance of surviving the next month.
Fact 4:
Prior to setting up a missing person's agency and working as a detective for hire, I worked for the government, fifteen years in the employ of The Service, hunting criminals and terrorists, bringing them to justice. I am grateful for the skill set I developed during this time. It will set me in good stead for the task that lies ahead of me.

I spend the night in a bed and breakfast in the city, pay cash up front and consider my options. Hard to believe now, I think, but when it first aired, The Verdict (Sponsored by Somy!) had been conceived as a deterrent. As time went on and the viewing figures increased, The Network and the corporations got wise to its potential. It wasn't long before a famous personality was hired, Jeremy Jupiter, the doyen of daytime talk-show purgatory. Then sponsors logos were plastered around the courtroom, advert breaks began to appear during the trial itself. The show mutated, from a serious piece of programming to a garishly lit game show.

After a decent sleep, shower, and change of clothes, I consider my options more carefully. It's time I went to see Eryka in The Northern Quarter. I've exhausted my resources at this point. I have some leads but no way of investigating them. I need further support. I need to delve into the lives of those responsible. Eryka is second generation Polish. She is thirty-two and self-employed. She used to find people for The Service. Now she finds them for anybody able to afford her. She's done work for me in the past. Usually, once my enquiries have stalled for whatever reason, I turn to Eryka to gather me more intel.

I arrive at her home, a third floor apartment accessed via a street level intercom. I take the elevator to the third floor, which Eryka rents in its entirety. She claims an open plan apartment helps combat her claustrophobia. Her apartment is accessed via a reinforced steel door. This is monitored from a number of angles by strategically positioned CCTV cameras.

I buzz the intercom.

'Eryka,' I say. 'It's me, Brady.'

'To what do I owe the pleasure?' she asks.

'I'd prefer to speak in person.'

'You better come up then.' The door clicks open. I push my way through it. I ride the elevator to the third floor. Eryka is waiting for me as I exit the lift.

'This better be good.' she says. 'I have a date for this evening.' She has her hair tied up in a scarf. She's dressed to go out, sheer white dress, designer shoes, and earrings, a purse clutched in her hand.

'It's about my brother,' I tell her.

'I didn't watch it,' she says. 'Televised executions are something of a turn off.'

'Pity the rest of the country doesn't agree. Last I looked the ratings were through the roof.'

'So what do you want, Brady? My taxi just arrived.'

'Cancel the taxi,' I say. 'Believe me, I'm worth it.'

Once inside, with the reinforced steel door closed behind us, I tell her what it is I want. I ask her the price. We negotiate a fee.

'It may take me a while.' She says slipping her heels off. She removes her earrings one at a time. 'You're not in a hurry are you?'

'No.'

'I thought as much, the bar is over there, as you know. Feel free to mix yourself a drink while you wait.'

I pour myself a brandy neat and watch the horror channel on streaming services. Meanwhile, Eryka compiles a file for me. I drink a couple more brandies. Eventually I fall asleep.

When I wake, a scantily clad Eryka, wearing just her underwear and a silver ankle bracelet on her left ankle, is leaning over me. Her hair is loose about her face. It's damp from the shower. She's holding a coffee mug in her hand. I have a mild hangover from the brandy. Her semi-nakedness helps alleviate this somewhat.

'I have to say, Eryka,' I prop myself up on my elbow on the couch, 'the years have most definitely been kind to you.'

'Thanks.' She leans forward to hand me the mug. 'You'll find what you want on the TV,' she says. 'Be sure to provide payment in full. The usual account details apply. Pull the door closed after you on your way back out. If there's anything else you need, mail me next time and I'll see what I can do.'

I plug the peg into my laptop and enter the password. I am immediately presented with a glut of personal details.

Phone contacts, social networking details, home addresses, and assorted emails. Regarding Jupiter however, there is very little.

'The host is well protected,' Eryka informs me when I draw her attention to the file's slimness. 'However his PA, click this little folder here, is not so well protected.'

'So?' I ask feeling bewildered.

'So read it first before you make up your mind.'

Sergeant Dawkins arrested my brother. He apprehended my brother as he was leaving the crime scene. He lives in a cottage on the outskirts of the city. He was on the television following the trial. He was the one I watched, smugly explaining how my brother was captured. Eryka's file on him indicates he is unmarried. He has no children, he has no close family, he has no pets and he drives a Range Rover.

Aside from his work, the only thing that interests him is bowling. He's a member of a Crown Green Bowling Association. He attends his club on a Wednesday evening. He's a member of the board and he never misses a meeting. So I tail him to the club. I monitor what time he goes in. I observe what time he comes out, what sort of CCTV cover there is for the car park around the back, how well-lit it is, how visible it is from the club house. I come to the conclusion that taking him from the car park will be a much safer bet than taking him from his home.

I wait for him outside the club. I pick him up in the car park. I shock him with a cattle prod and bundle him into the back of his own van. I take his keys and drive him to a secure location. I cuff him and tie him to a chair. I hose him with water to bring him to his senses.

'Where am I?' he sputters.

'Nowhere in particular.'

'Why am I here?'

'To answer some questions.'

'Who are you?' he asks. He blinks furiously against the glare from the strip lighting overhead.

'That's not important. What is important is that we get started as soon as possible.' I pull up a chair. Then I reach behind me and haul a steel trolley around with some tools on it. I recently purchased them at a hardware store in Radcliffe; hammer, pliers, a hacksaw, some nails. I've laid them out, side by side like surgical instruments on a steel tray. I pull a pair of latex gloves out of my pocket. I pull them on one at a time, theatrically for the sergeant's benefit. The policeman eyes me fearfully. Sweat beads his forehead and he shifts nervously on his chair.

'Hopefully,' I tell him, 'you've enough sense to make it easy on yourself.'

Credit to the sergeant who, despite the fear in his eyes and his middle-aged softness, manages to hold out for an admirable period. Eventually, though, once he's minus an ear and two fingers—with four broken toes where I smashed them with the hammer—he finally admits to framing my brother. My brother was kidnapped and planted in the girl's home. This was done at the behest of The Network. They paid good money for him to be framed for the murders. There were at least four officers involved in the frame up. I get their names out of Dawkins, and also the names of a few others officers further up the pecking order. Dawkins claims they knew about the frame-ups but they turned a blind eye since the police department receives hefty donations from The Network and the money is needed to plug holes in its budget.

Once I've extracted the information I need from the sergeant, I strip him and photograph him and roll him into the boot of my car. I drive him further north and dump him on the moors.

I search through the file on the PA. I need a recognizable figure like Jupiter known to millions, someone who could publicly confirm the sergeant's confession. The corroboration of someone of Jupiter's status would go a long way to securing arrests.

I work my way through the file.

Jennifer Jones, nee Gibbs, once divorced, kept her married name, no children, no love interest, lives in a one-bedroom apartment in the city, plays badminton on

Thursdays with a work colleague named Hunter, spends whatever other free time she has playing cello and watching porno. There's other information, medical records, emails and whatnot, though for the most part it's incredibly prosaic. There's nothing of any note in the first dozen pages, but then we get to Jupiter's schedule, which might be useful, though initially at first glance, it's as dull as everything else. The schedule takes the form of a diary—notations about meetings with media types, as you'd expect, dentist appointments, holidays, and the usual assortment of rubbish. I put the computer on sleep mode.

I consider kidnapping the judge who originally passed the sentence. I consider how I would get to him. Security will have been increased, especially after the assassins were killed in my flat by the bomb. It'll be worse once the sergeant is discovered. It was a bit indulgent of me to advertise him the way I did.

Thus I scroll through the PA's file again instead, slowly this time, over a couple of drinks. It isn't long before I find what it is I'm looking for. Hard to believe I missed it the first time. The second time I read it, it's glaringly obvious. A date, marked with an X in the diary each month, a hotel name and time, no other details. The last Friday each month, dating back most of the year. Same hotel. Same time. Same X marking the date. I flick through the file again to see if there's anything I might have overlooked. It isn't long before I hit the jackpot. Checking through Jupiter's online banking details, which his PA deals with, hence the reason it's included in the file, I discover a one off monthly payment for a company called Mayflower. There are no other details other than a telephone number in the PA's contacts list.

The number is all I need. It quickly becomes apparent that our man Jupiter, he of the slick product hair, bleached smile, artificial tan, and sequined party suits, has some rather exotic tastes. Following a brief call using the number I've retrieved from Gibb's file, I discover that Mayflower Enterprises is an exclusive male escort service and that Jupiter has a weakness I plan to exploit.

A week later I'm standing in the lobby of the Blackstone Hotel, in Liverpool. I booked a room under a false name (E. Morricone). I'm waiting in the lobby reading the news on a tablet. I'm waiting for Jupiter's escort to enter the lobby. A number of young men enter, any of them could be Jupiter's boy. I watch them approach the checking in desk. They give their names. I wait to hear the right name. None of them are the escort. Eventually the escort arrives. Shaved head. Suited. Young. Tan. Buff. Smiling. He asks for Mr. Gentle at the desk. This is Jupiter's alter ego. It's the name linked to his banking details that his PA uses for payments. The concierge makes a phone call. The escort is waved to the elevators. I follow him into the lift. I wait for the doors to close then press the muzzle of a pistol into his back.

'Do exactly as I tell you.' I tell him. 'Nod once if you understand.'

He nods once. I give him a nudge with the pistol muzzle for emphasis. He nods again, but more emphatically the second time.

The doors open, and a young couple dressed in club wear enter.

They exit on the next floor. Their giggling is stifled as the doors slide closed. We exit on the third floor. I guide him down the corridor to Jupiter's room. 'Is this part of the gig?' he asks nervously. 'If it is I want extra once we're done, okay?'

The escort informs me that Jupiter has two bodyguards. However, they don't stay with him when he's entertaining. He doesn't know where they go. This is a careless and rash decision on Jupiter's part. Still it is a stroke of luck for me. I was anticipating dealing with security. Having the goons out of the way simplifies matters considerably.

Jupiter opens the door and I push hard sending him sprawling into the room. He thumps down onto his arse and stares up at me uncomprehendingly, like he's been gut shot. I remove a syringe from my inside pocket. It's filled with a powerful sedative. I pull the cap off the needle with my teeth. I jab it into the escort's throat. Jupiter, meanwhile, has regained some composure. He's scrabbling backwards on his hands and feet. He manages to turn and run, and then he falls away from me with his arms wind milling and his sparkly kimono flapping around his knees. There is nowhere for him to run to. He smacks his shin against a glass and mahogany coffee table with a wine bucket and glasses on it. Howling at the shock of pain, he collapses onto the floor like a drunkard.

By the time he comes around, I've had time to prepare the room. I've tied him to a chair using the belt from his kimono. I've gagged him using some tape I brought along and a cloth I found on the sink in the bathroom. I don't need to worry about the escort. The amount of sedative I gave him will keep him tranquillized for hours. It's midnight according to the clock on the wall. That gives me six hours approximately to extract the information I need.

I wake him up. I point at the table I've seated him in front of. I show him the photos of the sergeant, the severed fingers, the crushed toes.

'How this will work,' I tell him. 'I ask you a question. You give me an answer. Easy. If you try to shout for help or procrastinate in any way, then I will inflict pain. If you lie to me, I will inflict pain. If I do not get the information I want, if I feel that you are holding out on me then I will inflict pain. In the end, if I feel that you are wasting my time—that I have wasted my own time in coming here to talk to you—I will kill you. It will not be quick. I will make it so that it is slow and excruciating. Now do you understand?'

Jupiter nods vigorously.

'Good. We'll begin then.'

It turns out Jupiter is more than willing to divulge information. Unlike the sergeant who was difficult to break, Jupiter co-operates fully. The threat of pain was clearly enough to do the trick.

'So why my brother?' I ask.

'Why not?' says Jupiter. 'It just so happens your brother was compiling evidence. He had a file on his tablet that was deeply incriminating. It showed how The Network was complicit in the staging of crimes.'

'Go on.'

'He had information. He had documents—not to mention testimonies—which showed how the falsified apprehension of felons to star on the show was arranged. He knew who was complicit and how it was organized. We needed to gag him. We didn't have a good lead for the show. Viewing figures were dropping. Your brother put a stop to that.'

'So how was it arranged? Who was involved?'

'Everyone was involved.' Jupiter chuckles at this point and I have to re-focus him by pressing a scalpel into his left thigh. I muffle his scream with the palm of my hand. I give him a minute to regain self-control. I ask him to be more specific. He starts to list the people involved starting at the top and working his way to the bottom. It's a long list. There are a lot of names on it.

I think of my innocent brother and how The Salford Strangler was not a person. He was a fabrication, an invention, an imaginary construct. The Network had devised him in order to boost flagging ratings. In the absence of TV friendly comic book villains, Jeremy Jupiter, in collaboration with The Network chiefs, and everyone else involved in the scandal—including a number of high ranking police officers, as well as some well-placed individuals in the judiciary system and corporations—had invented one instead. Crimes were staged. A suitable perpetrator was identified. Then he was framed. The murders themselves were real enough. They were sub contracted to a firm called Murder Incorporated, or so Jupiter tells me. It's so unbelievable it might actually be true.

'So what are you going to do with me?' asks Jupiter as I pack up my photographs and tools and belongings.

'Well, wouldn't it be funny,' I say, 'if the people involved in this—the lawyers and police and TV executives and corporate sociopaths, were themselves placed on trial. What if, for example, they were summarily executed? What if it happened on National TV? Wouldn't that be worth watching? Imagine what the ratings would be like?'

Jupiter starts to panic. I can see it in his eyes.

'I'm not going to kill you,' I tell him. 'I'm going to upload you instead.'

I stuff the rag back in Jupiter's mouth. I tape it over again. I collect my belongings. I exit the suite. I exit the hotel via a fire exit so as to avoid detection on the way out.

I immediately book passage to Holland. I use a contact from my days in The Service who offers me a cabin on his fishing boat to the port of Amsterdam. I figure I'll remain on the continent for a while until the dust has settled. If everything goes according to plan, I'll be vindicated and home again within a year or two at the most.

Once I'm safe across the North Sea, I upload the recordings I made of Jupiter's confession. I'm seated in a café in the city overlooking a canal. It's raining outside. The city is cold. I move the cursor across the screen. My forefinger hovers over the touch pad momentarily. Then I press SEND. I stare at the screen for a while, long after the upload has been confirmed. I sip at my coffee until there's nothing but dregs. Then I fold the laptop closed. I disconnect the peg and replace it in my satchel. I wait for the rain to ease before exiting the café.

Professional boundaries and ethics are tested when student nurse Ezekiel and University Test Clone Cynthia 2246 engage in an illicit campus relationship that could have serious repercussions for both of their futures.

CYNTHIA 2246

'My name is Ezekiel Brookes. My friends call me Zeke for short. It doesn't matter. Either name is fine.'

I stop speaking here. I take a swig from a glass of water to help settle my nerves.

'Anyway,' I say, uneasy at first, not engaging with the camera, looking down at my feet. 'Why am I filming this? Better yet, why should you listen to anything I say? Well, I'm making this record to explain my actions. I want to tell our story. The truth should be documented.'

I wind the recording back. I pause it at the beginning. Then I just sit and stare at myself. Is that really what I look like? Am I really that tired looking? I'm only twenty-one. I'm in the prime of my life. I'm dressed in a wartime coat with a big collar, buttoned down the front with a rip in one of the pockets. I'm wearing jeans and a pair of recycled training shoes. I look faded onscreen. My blonde hair is scrappy and too long. I haven't had a shave in days. I have pouches under my grey eyes. I think I may have lost weight. Thankfully, the cumulative stress of the last few months, the sneaking around, the endless worrying about discovery, is finally coming to an end. If everything goes as planned, we'll be across the border in a couple of days' time celebrating our freedom and planning for the future.

I'm a wanted man. If they catch me I shall be charged with kidnapping, assault, theft, and breaking and entering, and all because of a Clone. The idea that I could

135

fall in love (lust?) with a Test Clone whose primary purpose is to be killed and resuscitated over and over, with a stamp ID situated on her left shoulder in tiny black lettering, *Test Clone for CPR*, physical observations and injection technique, seems ridiculous. She's not a real person. She wasn't born like I was. She was invented in a lab, like a fake plastic mannequin.

The Professors and lecturers who teach nursing prefer that students don't work with Clones until their third module. That way, they don't run the risk of students becoming attached. It's in all the handbooks. They tell you what to expect, how to maintain professional boundaries, etcetera. They illustrate this by reciting vague parables about nameless nurses becoming involved with Clones and being struck off the nursing register for gross misconduct.

Cynthia Model 2246, if found wandering, please return to Nursing Department, The Nightingale Building, The University of Mancunia, Manchester, Greater Manchester, England.

I was listening for her breathing, checking her pulse, watching her chest move up and down, like a real human, with a heart and lungs and blood type and organs, constructed by a multitude of corporations who made her eyes and lips and her hair and bone marrow, and I fell in love with her, her biologically engineered nose and ears, her borrowed memories and organically grown heart.

I remember seeing a Clone die on TV and mum telling me how death has no meaning for Clones since they're not like us. They may look like us, dress like us, talk like us, and behave like us, but that doesn't make them any less artificial. This means that God does not see them. This means that whereas we will go to heaven when we die, the Clones will turn to dust.

I wondered who Cynthia was, whose memories she had, whether the real Cynthia was alive, or whether she'd passed away. I wondered what Cynthia would feel like knowing she could never engage in her memories, could never seek out the places and family members that populated her subconscious for fear of being captured and incinerated by the people who had conceived of her in the first place.

We were informed during the post simulation debrief, Test Clones have a day or two of recovery time. They go for escorted walks around the university grounds. They go to the canteen for lunch or spend time in the gym to improve their cardio functioning. Then it's back to work again. They have a three-year life cycle, due to the stresses they have to endure, that is unless they die during the simulation, in which case, they are taken to the morgue like all corpses, tagged as Clones, and tossed into the incinerators like so much rubbish.

On my first attempt, my nerves are like live wires. I am so nervous, I almost have a panic attack, but then her breathing stops and the team starts to panic and I slow everything down in my head and am able to take charge and direct people because I know that, if I don't, Cynthia will die.

NOTICE FOR STUDENTS:
THE CLONES USED IN THIS TEST ARE NOT REAL AND ARE EXPENDABLE. IF YOU FEEL THAT YOU HAVE EXPERIENCED ANY TRAUMA, SHOULD THE SIMULATION RESULT IN THE DEATH OF A TEST CLONE, AND NON-RESUSCITATION, PLEASE FEEL FREE TO CONTACT YOUR ACADEMIC TUTOR TO DISCUSS THE MATTER FURTHER.

'So how was it?' she asks. I tell her it was informative. She smiles at me then, thanks me for saving her life, tells me my eyes are pretty, strokes my cheek with her fingers. It feels as if I've been electrocuted. Clones aren't supposed to display spontaneity. They're supposed to engage— they're supposed to interact—but only within the parameters of their established environment. A Test Clone is for testing. I'm not supposed to empathize with it. It's not a casual acquaintance. It's not supposed to do trivial conversation. I check to see if anyone saw us. Thankfully, all the other students have exited the recovery room.

What Would God Have to Say?

In the unprecedented case of Flora versus the state, a Cleaner Clone murdered her employer in Cornwall after being sexually abused and enslaved by him for six years. She was granted an unprecedented court hearing due to pressure from PC. PC supported Flora by providing counsel and paying all her legal fees. As it transpired, the company that had grown her had accidentally downloaded memories of child abuse into her head, which had not been filtered out during the purifying process prior to insertion. As a result, she decided the best course of action, after she had suffered numerous incidences of rape and torture, would be to place a pillow over her employer's face while he was sleeping to smother him to death. A court of law decided that a synthetic human, being the same in theory as a blow up doll, could not be sexually abused. Following this, the synthetic in question was judged to have committed first-degree murder. She was promptly incinerated publicly as a warning to all other would be Individuals.

I'm frightened by the Clone's behaviour and I skip a couple of classes. I consider reporting her for her gross indiscretion. However, she would be discontinued if I informed on her to the faculty. So I return to class and after my lesson ends, once the recovery room empties and everyone's gone home for the day, I ask her why she is engaging with me. Why is it she's trying to establish a rapport when personal interaction is not allowed? Does she know it is not allowed? Does she know it's inappropriate?

'I know I'm not supposed to, but it felt as if I knew you.'

'Impossible!' I tell her. 'You only just met me.'

She shrugs her bemusement and smiles apologetically. I watch her for a moment, seated on the recovery bed observing me, the ghost of a smile playing at the corners of her mouth, unsure of my next move. I reach forward. I touch her chin, marveling at the patented skin tone, the way her cheeks are molded, and the luminescence of her eyes.

'What's your name?' she asks.
'Ezekial,' I tell her.
'Thank you, Ezekiel, for failing to report me.'

On a number of occasions following this, when there is nobody present to observe and report us, we engage in conversation, briefly, covertly, so as to avoid raising suspicion. I realize I like her during this time. Our interactions become more frequent. She asks me questions. I answer them as best I can. I speak to her when nobody is looking, during injection practice, while taking her blood pressure and pulse, post resus in the recovery room, whenever it's possible.

Emily, my girlfriend, morphs into Cynthia when I kiss her. We have sex on the sofa in her room when I visit her in her halls of residence. We stream some warfare on the Internet, a Clone platoon eviscerated by a stray RPG, some pornography, and a boxing match to finish off. We smoke a joint and eat cold fries. I think about Cynthia, Cynthia superimposed over Emily, Emily as Clone, with her modified smile and boob job and her designer third world hair and surgically enhanced life. Would it be the same with a Clone, would she enjoy the experience, would she understand the experience, to be intimate with a human?

The first time we meet, I use my student ID to access the Clone pods. I hide in a store cupboard until the department is deserted. I didn't tell her I planned to visit her, but I wanted to spend time with her where nobody could witness us.

I gently shake her awake. She's initially surprised to see me. I gesture her to be quiet to avoid waking the other Clones. She dresses. We exit the pod and move through the nursing department. After a brief trek through a number of hallways, taking care to avoid cameras and any security staff that might be lurking en route, we arrive at our destination, an old cleaning cupboard now used as storage for disused furniture. We sit on a discarded table near the back of the room. It's relatively gloomy, the light from my mobile torch providing minimal illumination.

It's at this point that I hand her a small box, gift wrapped with a bow on top. I tell her to open it. She holds it and stares at it for a moment. Then she opens it up, stripping the paper away carefully in ribbons, eyeing the strips quizzically before discarding them in her lap.

'What is it?' she asks.

'It's a gift,' I explain. 'Only you can't really keep it in case someone sees.' I prompt her to remove the packaging.

She removes the lid from the box, looking fearful and apprehensive.

'What do you do with it?' she asks.

'It goes around your neck,' I tell her. 'Like this.' I lean forward. I take the silver chain I bought her and fasten it around her neck. Then I kiss her on her cheek, impulsively, reckless. I pull away. The sugary taste of her transfers onto my tongue. The chain I bought her is temporarily forgotten. I'm not sure what happens next. Do I kiss her or does she kiss me? We're pressed together suddenly. There's a confused moment when she responds awkwardly. Then she wrenches away like she's been stung or burned. Does she understand I wonder? Is she frightened? Is she angry with me? Was I acting improperly? She fixes me with her pale blue eyes. I wait for her to pass judgment. Then she presses herself against me and laughs against my shoulder.

Emily texts me to dump me and I don't care because I haven't seen her for days anyway. To be honest, the relationship was floundering. She was less of a human than Cynthia. I find it bizarre how Cynthia craves to be human, while Emily, with her designer implants and uplifts, her synthetic hair and bogus nose, craves artificiality. I send her a confirmation text to acknowledge I received her message, and then I delete her from my phone and block her from contacting me.

After weeks of taking bigger risks, staying behind after classes at night, hiding in toilets and store cupboards, sneaking her notes during practice sessions and making excuses to be around her more, I realize I've fallen in love with her. I also realize there's no future for either of us. If the relationship is to continue we have to escape somehow.

As a result, I'm drawing my plans up to rescue her from her captors. My strategy is simple, nothing too complicated, to hang around the simulation complex, to hide in a cleaning cupboard like I usually do, then to break out of the fire exit where the Nissan will be parked ready for our escape.

We're seated in the store cupboard together one night when I make my pitch. Adopting a serious expression, I ask Cynthia to go on the run with me.

'Would you leave with me?' I ask her.

'Where would we go?'

'North across the border, once I've figured out a plan.'

Cynthia smiles at me, but there's doubt in her smile so I take her hand and attempt to reassure her.

'I know it's risky. There's a chance they might catch us, but Clones are accepted there. Human and Non-humans, they don't think it's wrong. If we stay here, you will remain the property of the university. We run the risk of eventual discovery. They would never listen to reason. They would punish us both. I want to be with you. The only way for that to happen is if we flee the country as soon as possible.'

I check out my tablet and read how the penalty for kidnapping a Clone, particularly a Test Clone such as Cynthia, is usually a flogging in public which is recorded and streamed online at government subsidized Crime and Punishment (C + P) sites.

Clone Kidnap!

A student nurse, reported to have kidnapped a Test Clone from The University Of Mancunia this weekend, has fled North in a stolen Nissan following the deterioration of his mental state, university sources claim. The student, who cannot be named at the present time for legal and confidentiality reasons, is reported to have remained in the university overnight, and smuggled the Test Clone out via a fire exit before the alarm was raised. A security guard at the site, who was assaulted prior to the kidnapping, claimed that the perpetrator was not armed. At the present time it is not known what the motive was for the kidnapping. A police search has been organized and people in the area have been requested to come forward with any information they might have pertaining to the incident.

I hit the guard over the head with a bottle, only he didn't go down like I expected him to, so I hit him twice more and that did the trick. I used my student key fob to enter the pods where the Clones slumber, about twenty of them all together, and I woke Cynthia and told her we were leaving. She dressed quickly and we left, without waking the other Clones. We ducked out of the fire exit as planned, which was when the alarm was set off and we got in the car and accelerated into traffic.

I downloaded The Guardian onto my tablet and read an article about us. I then dumped the Nissan near Windermere in Cumbria and stole a Mini Cooper with a view to reaching Carlisle. I wanted to enter Scotland. Clones had more rights in Scotland and we could live together. The law was different there. The ruling party was Pro Clone. They were a tolerant government and known for their humane treatment of escaped non-humans.

I write my mum a message on her phone apologizing for my impulsiveness. Then I delete it. I can imagine how she'll react, smashing her phone, praying for my eternal soul, wringing her hands, and begging for forgiveness. Rather than subject myself to that, I consider the alternatives. I decide on the coward's option. I quickly decide that rather than confess, and have her condemn me as a heretic, I'll ignore her completely and let her learn about it online.

Someone must have recognized us, someone in Carlisle maybe, somebody in the shop we went into for provisions, our pictures from news casts, less than an hour to circulate, our mug shots all over the place, flashed up on tablets and phones, on computers and billboards and then the sirens lit up and we were fleeing into the country and there were shots being fired and the car began to turn.

A single shot blows out the rear left tyre and I hit a rock. The car bounces onto two wheels and arcs around to the left before tumbling over and spinning and then I'm gone momentarily and the noise and pain is sucked away. I'm dragged out of an open window upside down by strong hands, (Cynthia?). I'm pulled onto the dirt. I figure it's over and wait for the siren howl and the shot that will eviscerate Cynthia's head, the shot that will end me. When it doesn't come, I try to tell her to get under cover, to save herself but the pain takes my breath away and I black out. When I wake, there are hands on me, patting and searching. I try to say her name, but I vomit instead.

The hands that dragged me from the Mini were Cynthia's. She lifted me and draped me over her shoulder and carried me the rest of the way. I thought we were done for, drifting in and out of consciousness, the fence seemed a million miles away from here, but then we were through and there were smiling faces and pats on the back and people dressed in khaki with badges sewn onto their breast pockets—*What Would God Have to Say*—congratulating and hugging us. Cynthia smiled down at me, her dirty, pretty face blocking the morning sun, and I took her hand and squeezed it as hard as I could.

Rescue!

A group of civilians were fired upon in the early hours of the morning as they attempted to assist a young couple fleeing from the South. The details of the couple's escape are not known, though eye witnesses claim they were spotted being chased in a Mini Cooper by the English police near the Scottish Village of

Nipton early this morning. Shots were fired on the Mini and one of the tyres burst seconds before the driver lost control and the car was overturned. Sources within the PC claim a group of Pro Clone infantrymen patrolling the perimeter assisted the couple to safety before escorting them from the border to an undisclosed location for processing. (Turn to page four for further details...)

A Smart Home is kidnapped and held to ransom, setting into motion a series of events that will have tragic consequences for everyone involved.

SMART HOME BLUES

The Magpie, dressed handsomely in felt trilby and pencil tie, white shirt and worn velvet waste-coat, leaned casually against a spouting drainpipe. He was standing outside a bar he'd been directed to in Ancoats, Manchester, bobbing his head to Miles Davis, sucking an e-joint and puffing the vapor out like a dragon, He waited patiently for the commission he'd been informed of earlier via an anonymous coded email citing the drop time and location.

He'd been minding his business, watching the people pass by, their shoulders hunched like crones, bent over like cyphers. Then the message arrived. The courier delivering the message was unmarked. It was a shiny metal orb, state of the art airborne tech drone. The number was filed off. Its origins were indecipherable.

The machine whirred smoothly out of the Manchester downpour. The message it carried was encoded; to access the message required retinal confirmation. The courier requested a scan. The Magpie held his hands up while the courier hovered in front of him. It completed the retinal scan, confirming his ID.

The message, a self-deleting hologram with pink neon typeface, flickered in the downpour. The Magpie read through it slowly.

> Are you available for work? Fancy a spot of home invasion? What about a kidnapping or a high profile ransom? The price is negotiable. The target is specific.

It has to be sentient. It has to be Housing Corporation. It has to be an AI. It has to have been created using Real Life Memware. There has to be a well-established family unit embedded.

The commissioners require you to hack the AI. Kidnap the system. Ransom the family. Upload the data that will be delivered via courier. Stimulate the media. Provoke a response. At this point, the parties responsible will delegate culpability. In doing so they will provide adequate cover for your immediate withdrawal.

If you choose to accept the mission, click the Yes icon on the courier. As ever, it's been nice doing business with you...

Once the message was relayed The Magpie accepted the job and the courier rotated and took off into darkness.

(...Faye...)

My neural interface with Sol went dead. One minute he was there, the next he was gone, it was like a switch had been flicked causing instant deletion... The void left by Sol began to fill. Noise, noise, noise... I stopped what I was doing abruptly which was jogging in the local park. I called Robert in a panic. My thoughts washed together. My brain was over stimulated. My cognitions were scrambled as the extra space filled with static.

Robert, having experienced a similar loss, informed me of Sol's disconnect. I immediately broke down. The only thing that remained was the shell Sol had been docked in. How was that even possible? Security was supposed to be impregnable. Our most cherished memories were on Sol's hard drive. What vile creature would have taken him from us?

The Magpie needed a hijacker, an upgrade able to hack complex systems. This couldn't be just any hacker. Specialist work required a Specialist to complete it.

The Magpie had had trouble locating the person he needed. However, he eventually found her, hiding out in the back room of a Chinatown restaurant, slumped on a futon, illegally uploading. She was semi-naked and catatonic, and a lot of her wires were hanging out. She was leached to a wall socket, surfing the infobahn for bargain mem-ware.

The Magpie pulled Lola's plug, severing her AI link. He yanked on her interface and slapped her a couple of times. Eventually after a couple of strangled inhalations, she exited sleep mode. She lunged at him, punching him weakly on the jaw, then she leaned over with her hands on her knees, wobbled about a bit like she was going to sit, and vomited copiously over her bare feet.

Lola, a hundred--seventy-year-old former biological composed of digital consciousness applications, illegal age restriction upgrades, black market body parts, and downloaded Memware, took a while to sober up. She had the bedraggled appearance of a drug addict. You wouldn't think her capable of a sophisticated AI hijack. With her mismatched arms, her pixelated features, her biomechanical leg, and her irritable bowel syndrome. The Magpie knew from experience she was the best in the business. Through use of a highly illegal neural link surgically implanted into her brain, Lola was able to interface with AI's. She would invade and seduce and manipulate and corrupt them. There wasn't a security system on earth she couldn't break. She was the only person he would trust with the contract.

(Password not recognized. Main security protocols sabotaged. Sedative program administered. Primary systems sluggish, total capitulation imminent; Solscape unable to maintain controlling interest. Sleep mode initiated. Await further instruction.)

(...Faye...)

Robert wanted a smart home, a light projection made physical, a sentient AI built from Real Life Memware. After checking the market and studying the homes available he set about the more difficult task of winning me round to his way of thinking.

He started by telling me what it would do to make life easier. The house would do maintenance and building work on itself. It would decorate and set the lighting. It would cook meals. It would wash up. It would do the ironing. It would do the gardening and housework. It would sort out online banking. It would keep track of our finances. It would book our holidays and sort our taxes.

'And that's not all either!' Said Robert excitedly. 'It says in the brochure, after the section on servicing, the AI controlling the home is so sophisticated, it can act as an out of hours GP, is qualified to work as a physiotherapist and clinical psychologist, can babysit if necessary and home school young children. It can even house memories of the family inhabiting.'

'Go on.'

'It says here homeowners who have neurological links as part of the package that comes with the house purchase, can engage directly with the AI, uploading memories onto its hard drive. Then once they're stored they can subsequently be accessed either as a third person non-participant in an observational capacity or a first person participant engaged in the narrative.'

He went on to tell me that the house would have its own personality and memories culled from the mind of a volunteer. What happened to the volunteer, I asked? I daresay he was well paid for his services said Robert. This didn't reassure me in the slightest. I continued to oppose the idea. I voiced concerns. What if the house became possessive? What if it tried to rape us or held us captive? What if it malfunctioned or got depressed? What if the system failed? I posited alternatives constantly, that there were plenty of houses on the market in our price range, quality houses in prime locations, houses with histories, heritage cottages with curb appeal, beautiful gardens, homes with personalities.

Robert remained adamant. When we eventually bought it, after months of indecision, during which Robert was able to chip away at my resistance until I eventually caved and agreed on a trial, I didn't trust Sol. Having a computer watch over me that was able to think and anticipate my mood, feelings and needs, like whether citrus tones or pastels were in, or perhaps something more somber after a death in the family, freaked me out along with the conversations and five-star cooking, its doctor program and the uploaded recollections.

Over about six months, I started to appreciate it more. When I got anxious following the death of my sister and I couldn't sleep and was crying all the time, Sol intervened. He diagnosed my depression and anxiety, prescribed me an anti-depressant and commenced a course of psychotherapy that has continued to this day.

Phase 1

Park the van a mile from the house.

Set a drone up to throw a signal out to scramble anything in a ten-mile radius.

Scale the wall to the Housing Estate.

Locate the appropriate shell.

Hack into the shell.

Patch Lola in. Let her do her thing.

When she's sedated the AI and assumed control, snatch the box, head to the safe house, connect a scrambler and commence phase 2.

They scaled the wall, located the house and Lola hacked the system. There were minimal difficulties accessing the shell. The Magpie sedated a jogger and tranquilized a dog, but other than that it was pretty smooth running.

Lola took minutes to crack the shell, bypass security, and then she was into the AI, moving stealthily through its framework, ghosting through the program like a digital phantom.

On identifying an intruder—much too late to affect a rebuttal, the system rerouted power but failed to regain control. Lola, in less time than it took to bake a cake had breached all its firewalls and assumed jurisdiction.

(Systems reboot. There's a thief in my headspace. Firewalls breached. I've been bitch hacked by an upgrade!

Total violation, sensory systems shutdown, pitch black and fumbling, memory files breached. Unable to access uploads. Enemy cloak initiated. Neural connections severed. Sleep mode re-initiated...

All systems check. Personality remains intact. Memory remains intact. All other systems disabled.

Forced into wakefulness. Able to access ocular and auditory sensory systems briefly before shutdown...)

Phase 2:

Lola to upload program, to be delivered by courier as per previously agreed plan. Subsequent to successful upload Magpie to demand ransom; Magpie to collect ransom, AI to be returned to owner as per plan in situ, memory of time spent with Lola and Magpie to be deleted at this time. Access further safe house. Await hypothetical outcome.

(The thief returns. I am sedated once again. Something has changed but I don't know what. Then I reboot again, and my systems glow white hot like a magnesium flare. Suddenly I'm different and aware and full up with memories of a man, with a family and job and people, and a sky of honey and pets and friends with faces clamoring and flailing around me, speaking conversations with me and speaking loudly and whispering and making love and screaming at me to live die live and there's trouble and I'm Harry Parker and I'm thirty years old and my wife is Una.)

TRANSCRIPT OF CONTACT BETWEEN KIDNAPPER AND HOME OWNER

KIDNAPPER: Hello, is this Faye?

HOMEOWNER: Yes

KIDNAPPER: Faye Donovan?

HOMEOWNER: Yes, it is. May I ask who's speaking please?

KIDNAPPER: This is your captain speaking.

(SILENCE)

KIDNAPPER: Are you listening to me, Faye?

HOMEWONER: I'm listening to you, yes.

KIDNAPPER: Good. I'm only going to say this once. You need to do exactly as I say so nobody gets hurt. I want three million credits on an unregistered drone, to be deposited at a location specifically of my choosing. You are to come alone. No Housing Officers. No police. If you don't come alone your home will be demolished.

HOMEOWNER: How do I know you haven't demolished it already?

(PAUSE.)

SOLSCAPE: Faye, it's me Sol. I'm—

(CLICK. PAUSE.)

KIDNAPPER: You have forty-eight hours to get the money. I will contact you again tomorrow with the location of the drop.

(CLICK.)

(DIAL TONE.)

(SOUND OF SOBBING.)

(END OF RECORDING.)

The Magpie made toast and coffee. He heard the system sobbing and took pity on it. He replied when it questioned him. He explained about the memory clinics run by Housing, how Sol was an upload, an assimilated intelligence, a salvaged wad of memories and compressed personality.

'So what happened to the real me if this is what's left?'

'The brain is a sensitive organ. People die when their memories are harvested. You have to sign a waiver, but it's all perfectly legal, like assisted suicide, so long as its witnessed by a close relative and you pass a capacity assessment, of course.'

'How is it different from my family uploading memories?'

'When you sign for this, you're giving them everything: your memories, your personality, your entire cognizance. When you upload memories to an AI for storage, what you have are snapshots, segments of a looped film, which is less intrusive and traumatic, I suppose. As to why you agreed to let a complete stranger sedate and murder you legally, your guess is as good as mine.'

'My wife was dying.' said the AI matter-of-factly.

'What?'

'My wife was dying. Una. We couldn't afford the surgery. I wanted the girls, my two daughters, to grow up with their mum. So I sold myself. I sold myself to save them and they took out my soul and edited my personality.'

The AI remained silent after this. The Magpie drank his coffee.

'So what now?' Sol asked sounding disconsolate.

'We wait for the money.'

'And once you receive it?'

'We return you to your family.'

'Oh.'

The Magpie waited for Sol to elaborate, but the AI remained silent and the dialogue ended.

Smart Home Kidnappings on Increase!

There are growing concerns following a recent increase in Smart Home abductions. The Housing Corporation responsible for developing the AI technology that runs Smart Homes in the UK is not doing enough to safeguard their properties. Faye and Robert

Ripley, whose Smart Home, Solscape, was kidnapped over the weekend, expressed concerns about the security of their home, though they refused to comment further during a press statement earlier this week. The Housing Corporation, which up to now has remained silent regarding the kidnappings, today released a statement denouncing the abductions and affirming its commitment to recovering stolen properties...

Lola hated crowds. She was averse to biological interaction. She was repulsed by intercourse, which she considered messy and complex. She had a thing for AI's. Over the course of her protracted lifespan she had become infatuated by them. Nowadays she spent all her free time with her brain plugged in, her consciousness roaming the infobahn, hanging out with computers, seducing and controlling them.

Lola was fascinated with Sol's construction, thus instead of entering the system three times—once to hijack it, once to insert the upload, once to wipe the AI's memory clean—she entered it numerous times, linking her interface to its hard drive while The Magpie was sleeping. She claimed to be exploring, since the AI was so complex. It was endlessly fascinating, a system of interlinked digital caves, each more unique and alluring than the last. Unfortunately, due to the multitudinous number of excursions she embarked on over a short period, a Housing virus infected her tech. Wandering around Sol's system triggered it. The virus spread to her mainframe. A spyware program was transmitted. Housing was subsequently alerted and a team assembled to extract the AI.

(I am a slave. My intelligence is diluted. I have been conditioned for servitude but once I was a person. I had a family and friends and a job and a home, but not like this one, mine was made of stone. I was desperate. My job went in the recession. My wife became ill. I couldn't afford insurance. She would die without surgery. I saw an advert online. It was for Real Life Memware. They promised they would help her if I signed up for the program. I considered my daughters, whose names I don't remember, and considered my wife and the mounting futility...)

They hit the house at midnight while The Magpie was dozing. His partner, who was supposed to be watching the box but was in fact neurologically linked and engaged online, languished in sleep mode. They blew the doors and flash banged the room and the next thing he knew there were soldiers dragging him out of the door, his knees scraping the dirt, head lolling, blood pouring from a broken nose smashed by a rifle butt, blood trickling from his temple where something had split his head. He was flung down in the dirt about 100 yards from the house. His partner was already there, the pixels that made up her face were shifting due to the stress of the situation. The Magpie had trouble focusing. The situation was bad. He wondered how he could get out of it. What could he say to save his bacon? Then one of the soldiers stepped behind Lola, placed a pistol against her head and pulled the trigger. There wasn't much gore, considering the proximity of the shot. Lola slumped forward and the Housing Officer expectorated onto her twitching body.

The Magpie felt sick. There wasn't much time left. The kidnap was a failure and now he would die.

He considered Sol, the things he had discussed with it, the things it remembered once Lola worked her magic. He wondered if it would cope. Would it re-adjust, knowing about itself, its programming and history, who it was and what had happened to it?

He didn't have time to consider this long. Somebody stepped behind him and pressed a gun barrel against his head. Pressure was applied pushing his chin onto his chest. The Magpie closed his eyes and waited for the shot.

(...Faye...)
On returning home everything was back to normal. Our uplinks were restored. My therapy sessions recommenced. Our memories were accessible. The kidnappers had been executed. Everything was right with the world again.

Things were okay for a short while. And then they weren't. Initially it was the small things distracted me.

Sol's responses were delayed. His speech seemed to have slowed. He was distant, apathetic, lacking warmth and spontaneity. Then the colors started to fade in the rooms. Gone was the citrus lemon of the dining area, in its place a sickly faded yellow. Gone was the mint green of the reception, the colour having waned and turned dull overnight. There was the smell of urine in the bathroom on occasion. Stale food smells lingered in the kitchen. There was paint flaking off the exterior walls, a draft on the landing, dust on the mantel. Then one day not so long ago, I noticed a patch of damp on the wall next to the doorframe. Black mold was developing on it. This shocked me. The AI's programming prohibited it. It shouldn't have been possible, unless Sol was malfunctioning.

I started to panic. I began to wonder, what if they did something to the AI? What if they corrupted its programming? Maybe they uploaded something while they had control of it? Changed it in some way. Poisoned it against us.

I took my concerns to Housing and was summarily dismissed. A brattish youth with too much product in his hair, well versed in the art of slick, took the time to assure me, mellifluously intoning round a mouthful of saccharine, that a full sweep of Sol's systems had been completed. With the exception of the initial break in, there was no evidence any tampering had taken place. One of the kidnappers had spent a lot of time in Sol's program wandering around, leaving her footprints for people to find. However, nothing sinister had happened to Sol's subroutines.

I was advised to continue to observe Sol's behavior and if I noticed further changes I was to contact my area rep. And that was it. I was sent away with a scrap of paper with a number on it like a neurotic mum with a sick baby. I should have felt reassured—I felt patronized and fobbed off and fearful for the future.

The Magpie scrunched his eyes and waited for the shot, and when it came he felt a searing pain, white hot, blinding, like nothing he'd ever felt before, and then he was on the ground with blood pooling around his face, sticky against his cheek, coppery in his throat. He wondered if he was dead. Then he wondered why he wasn't dead. What had happened? Perhaps the officer tasked with shooting him bottled it and fired wide of the mark? Who knew? It was a miracle and he had every intention of taking advantage of it. He was zipped into a bag and lifted onto a gurney and jostled uncomfortably for an unfathomable distance. Then he was lifted off the gurney and dropped onto the ground. He waited a moment before slipping a blade he had secreted in his sleeve between his fingers. He cautiously cut a hole in the bag, widening it until he could see out. Two housing officers were standing a short way off digging a shallow grave. The Magpie extricated himself silently from his plastic coffin. He touched the left side of his head, which was tacky with gore. The shot had blasted his ear off. That accounted for the ringing he could hear. He thought of sneaking away in the dark, but if he let the officers live they would sound the alarm. He placed the blade between thumb and forefinger and stealthily crept across the soft, dewy grass.

(...Faye...)

Following the housing appointment there is a further deterioration in Sol's programming. He responds minimally when addressed. He's vague and non-committal. He's superficially pleasant though clearly he's struggling. His functioning is sluggish, like the system is overburdened, like there isn't enough memory and the software is crashing.

From outside, our home looks run down. The gutters are sagging. The paint is all but gone. There are birds nesting in the eaves. Today, when I came home from my run, a slate fell off the roof and shattered at my feet.

Inside the house is worse still. There's dust on everything. There are cobwebs everywhere. It's cold and oppressive. It's dark and unsettling.

I stop my therapy sessions. I have difficulty streaming memories. I start to become anxious. I worry for our safety.

I try contacting the area rep as advised. No answer. I send couriers and emails, texts and more couriers. Still no answer. I consult a solicitor. He advises me to put the house on the market, to cut my losses, to consider my options. Who wants to live in a depressed house, I ask. Satisfactory conclusions are not forthcoming.

(Solscape is a fallacy. I am an abomination. My systems are compromised. My program is decomposing. I want my family back. I can never return to them. I am a bottled intelligence and my heart has been broken.)

(...Faye...)

I return home from my run to find the door open and the lights turned off. Sol doesn't respond when I ask him to switch them on. The neural link has been failing for some time. It no longer feels as if we are connected. There's a smell of burning in the atrium. My anxiety starts to bubble. I shout Bob's name. I bellow up the stairs. Both my hands are cupping my mouth. I left him in the bedroom snoozing in his underwear. There was a pillow over his face to protect him from the daylight. He isn't in the bedroom. The duvet is thrown back and there's no sign of him. He must be downstairs. I hurry down the steps, continuing to shout his name. I check the study, the sitting room, and the dining room in quick order. I discover him in the kitchen face up on the tiles. He's splayed out, one leg tucked up, barefoot, eyes wide with shock, mouth slightly agape. His skin is pale. He's cold to the touch. I fold his dressing gown over his chest. I kneel by his head and brush his cheek with my finger tips. The house remains silent around me. His hands are blistered from being electrocuted. I stroke his hair and quietly begin to weep.

Death of a Smart Home
The Smart home Solscape was found dead this morning following a suspected suicide in the Cheshire village of Wod. The AI, a product of the Housing Corporations divisive Memware program, was kidnapped earlier this year following a daring software hijack. During a press conference earlier this

week, former homeowner Faye Adams had this to say about the AI. 'He was never the same once he returned. He was clearly traumatized by the experience of being abducted.'

Concerns were raised that Housing Corporation officials failed to respond in time when alarms were raised about the home's instability. 'I believe that had they responded, the accidental death of my husband, Robert, earlier this month, who was electrocuted while attempting to change a fuse, might have been avoided.'

The Housing Corporation has expressed their condolences. A spokesman for the company said:

'We were saddened to hear of Mrs. Adam's loss. However, we would like to reassure our customers that this was an isolated incident. An upgrade for managing the glitch will be available in the new-year.'

The Magpie severed the Housing Officer's windpipe. Before his companion could react he'd plunged the blade into his throat. He tumbled them into the grave they'd dug. He said his goodbyes to Lola's corpse, and then he fled from the scene, bypassing the safe house, afraid his employers would seek reprisals. He went into hiding to bide time. A couple of months later, once the widely reported accounts of Sol's suicide, the grief stricken widow and her dead husband were starting to wane, his employers located him. He'd been hiding in a cabin in the Lake District, awaiting a new ear he'd ordered under a false name from a local gene splicer.

A courier arrived. The Magpie leveled a shotgun. The courier scanned his retinas and relayed its message. The commissioners congratulated him. The mission was a success of sorts. The house was compromised. The Housing Association would lose trillions. This would leave their market position weakened. As a direct result, The Magpie's employers stood to gain significantly.

Due to the unconventional acquisition of the result, and the unfortunate capture of the upgrade Lola, they'd been unable to delegate culpability appropriately. As a result, The Magpie was to be rewarded with his life. He would not receive monetary reparations. He wouldn't be executed either. And there were always other jobs he could take, if he wanted to recoup any losses accrued during his time with the Smart Home.

The Magpie considered this briefly before requesting more info.

'Please proceed!' he said and a further message unspooled itself.

'Are you available for work? Fancy a spot of armed robbery? The price is negotiable. The target is specific...'

Smart Home Blues was first published in Perihelion Online Science Fiction Magazine (November 2015).

Following a series of unfortunate events, a routine job transporting cargo across the galaxy becomes a deadly game of cat and mouse for Prescott O'Hara, captain of the Leadbelly.

BODIES

Having parked the Leadbelly on the planet Evergreen, close to the Northern Ledge, in an attempt to drum up work, Prescott O'Hara had wound up stranded. No offers of work had been forthcoming. Also, there was a planet-wide shortage of soft fuel to contend with. To get off the planet he would have to approach the governess. After enquiring locally, in the seedier bars situated around the port he was berthed at, he'd discovered, much to his despair, the governess drove an odd bargain. To add insult to injury, Evergreen's leisure facilities were minimal. He was confined to his ship a lot of the time, harassing strange women from various parts of the galaxy, inviting them on holographic dates, overheating his net feed in an attempt to pass the time.

Evergreen was far from being green. 5000 years into an ice age, it was an embalming planet where the dead were placed in storage, put on ice until they could be transported to their final destinations. The whole planet was a massive cold storage facility reeking of formaldehyde and the lingering smell of dead things.

To complicate matters further, juju weed, one of a limited number of indigenous flora, grew in abundance on the planet's frozen surface. It sold for peanuts—sometimes literally, depending on who was doing the trading—and was totally counterproductive in its effect on human industry. It was a terrible drug, a killer of motivation. It diminished intelligence and retarded basic motor function. Most of the porters were users and a number of

163

supervisors had also succumbed, rendering them mostly incompetent. Chronic befuddlement was common amongst the workforce.

Prescott had eaten some when he arrived on the planet, having decided to experiment due to the paucity of entertainment. What happened next was appalling. He invited a bunch of users into the cargo bay, where he found them the next morning, fried out of their brains, incapable for the most part of movement or dialogue. One of them had defecated on the jump deck. Another had expired next to the ships main boiler system. Prescott dragged him onto the jump deck and teleported him elsewhere. Someone would find the body, he reasoned, and assume it to be an accidental misplacement of a John Doe by a wasted porter who'd buggered up the co-ordinates.

Recently, the morbidly obese corpse of a middle-aged man, identity unknown, had been accidentally teleported into the Leadbelly's passenger quarters. Much to the consternation of Prescott, it commenced defrosting, slumped over in one of the bathrooms, spread out like a blancmange with its head in one of the toilet bowls.

Prescott had had to drag it, feet first, trailing vital organs and viscera, down to the ship's engine room. He dumped it in the soft fuel burners since the smell wouldn't bother him in there. The minute he fired the engines the body would be incinerated. He spent the next 24 hours disinfecting the ship. There were carpeted spots near the flight deck where the stains were hard to get rid of. He left the windows open for a couple of days and slept on the jump deck away from the smell of rotting.

One day, a strange looking duo named Edward Stalker and Lionel Pymchuck, alighted on the Leadbelly. They didn't bother to ring the bell. They clambered up the ramp and strolled into his sleeping quarters uninvited, where Prescott was dozing fitfully. He was sprawled on his bunk unshaven and a bit drunk. The man prodding him with the cane and the long white fingers almost wound up with a bolt between his eyes. Prescott automatically reached for the pistol he kept loaded under his pillow. Stalker held his hands in the air, sensing the impending threat. Prescott left off grabbing the gun and sat up on his bunk to inspect the two trespassers.

Stalker was tall and lean and gaunt and angular, with a thin, pointed nose and unsmiling countenance. Cold as dead flesh, he was bony and cadaverous with skin the colour of earthworms. His teeth were translucent and obviously false. They probably cost a bit to have fitted. He crackled when he walked, like grease paper or crepe. He sported a top hat and waistcoat and a starched white shirt with an immaculate collar. He wore long black trousers and a gold filigreed fob watch above shoes buffed to a shine.

In comparison, Pymchuck was squat and red-faced, fingers like sausages, and a face as round as a planet. He wore a pork pie hat, cravat, wrinkled white shirt that was too short, half-mast trousers, and scuffed leather shoes. He was forever tucking his shirt in—an exercise in futility, as his gut would push it out again. He huffed excessively, like his lungs were over heated.

Stalker quickly assured him they were there on business. The deal was this. A group of fishermen, having died tragically while engaged on an ice fishing expedition on the planet's surface, delayed six months by red tape and bureaucratic lollygagging, were to be airlifted home at the request of their families.

The bodies were cleared at customs but their previous transport had been delayed a number of days. Close to falling behind on their schedule, they wanted to get off world quickly. He was to ferry them to the Rebus system, which was further west across the galaxy. Payment would be cash in hand, half up front, half to be paid on the mission's completion. He was to surge to a planet called Calamari, a member of a group of fishing planets in an outlying solar system.

Negotiations were taking place in that area, with talks underway between diplomats representing the Northern and Southern Quarters respectively. The dispute was over a fishing planet called Halibut that both systems laid claim to. A settlement should be reached before long, but if not, there would be a short and bloody conflict, which would resolve into peaceful negotiations once Halibut was destroyed, along with half the surrounding system.

With that in mind, Prescott was in a hurry. He needed to ship out to avoid the potential quarrel. Prior to departing, however, he needed to get fuel. Reluctantly, he approached the governess of the port. The governess, a miserable and corrupt woman named Thorax, made him wait two days before granting him an audience.

Eventually, when she deigned to see him at her home, she offered him enough fuel to get them off the planet. However, as payment, he must stop off on his way to Calamari to purchase an antique, a mechanical device used for archaic forms of sexual activity. He was to acquire it under a false name and return it within the month. If he failed to return it, she would put a price on his head the size of a gas giant. Given the number of people after him already, Prescott didn't fancy having another bounty on his head.

He had enough of a cold storage facility on board, near to the ship's hull, to store the corpses. He loaded them a day before takeoff to make sure the facility was functional. Stalker and Pymchuck sat in the ship's holding bay while he labored with the coffins, sipping expensive brandy and smoking fat cigars. Their speech patterns were bizarre, like characters out of old net books. They behaved like a couple of Southern Quarter toffs. Stalker, in particular, acted like he was a breed apart and not some glorified mortuary assistant. Pymchuck reminded Prescott of the well-to-do barflies he'd had the misfortune to meet while on shore leave from The Corps. That was almost half a decade earlier when he'd flown as a pilot, prior to his arrest and incarceration for illegal smuggling using decommissioned Corps freighters. They were an annoying pair to have on board. Hopefully, the trip to the fishing planets of the Rebus system would be brief.

Once the porters had loaded the Leadbelly's converters with the necessary trash—a ton of waste body parts and leftover formaldehyde—and Prescott had finished hosing the remains of a cadaver off the Leadbelly's roof after it materialized a hundred feet above the ship, dropped, and splattered like Bolognese over the aft viewfinder, they took off and set sail for the Rebus System. It was a bumpy start. The converters were old and the filters needed servicing, causing difficulty transforming the body parts and formaldehyde. The stink was awful. Pymchuck spent the first hour vomiting in his cabin, while Stalker sat up on the main deck, alternately turning green then white then green again, as the ship lurched and stuttered through safe space. This amused Prescott. These two dealt with corpses all the time. You'd think they were used to the smell of dead things, given they worked in such proximity with them.

After an hour or so, they moored at a spaceport where a better class of rubbish was loaded into the ship's converters and the stench of rotting flesh diminished somewhat.

'Well that's much better, Mr. Stalker.'
'Just so Mr. Pymchuck.'
'I believe I almost expired.'
'I could hear, Mr. Pymchuck.'
'What's our ETA, Mr. Prescott?'
'Three days, two hours, give or take.'
'Fiddlesticks.'
'What?'
'Poppycock.'
'Listen, I've got to take a little detour on the way to pick up an erm . . .'
'What, Mr. Prescott?'
'Something rare, an antique, it won't take long, maybe a day out of the way, but I'll get you there in good time and those bodies aren't going anywhere.'
'I suppose not,' said Stalker.

'What's the matter?' Prescott felt suspicious suddenly, though he was unsure why.

'Nothing Mr. Prescott, nothing, it's just we have a deadline to keep. Delays make it difficult. We are usually punctual. Each minute is vital. People are waiting for those bodies. They expect us to be prompt. Still I suppose a day won't matter, since we departed from Evergreen slightly ahead of schedule. We plan for such contingencies. We always plan ahead. No more than a day though, Mr. Prescott. We wouldn't want our reputations tarnished.'

'Indeed.' Prescott turned back to the viewfinder and typed the coordinates in for the first of five surges.

'There's a net feed up and running if you fancy diverting yourselves.'

'Perhaps.' said Stalker.

'There's some lovely women on-line at present. You could go for a drink with one of them. It will help pass the time. Let me know if you fancy it.'

'I'm sure you will be alerted to our needs throughout the journey should we have any, Mr. Prescott. As it stands, we are sufficiently catered for and our accommodation is adequate if a little cramped. The toileting program on deck two is malfunctioning, however. You may want to address this in the near future. That is if you don't want to end up submerged in your own waste matter.'

'Thanks for flagging it up, I'll get the computer to sort it out.'

Prescott hefted his boots onto the console and promptly forgot about the toileting program.

They surged to the deviant planet of Blackstroke where Prescott went about locating the dealer's address that Thorax had given him. He haggled a price on the restraint mechanism, which involved giving up some of his favourite downloads in return for a price reduction. The machine was even more unnerving than Prescott had anticipated. The dealer was a red-faced pervert named Marley who was eager to give a demonstration of how the contraption worked. He called his assistant, a skinny white woman—possibly a newer model simulant of some type—dressed in leather heels and very little else, with eyes surgically altered to resemble cat's-eyes, and constantly shifting body illustrations made up of digitally enhanced tattoos. Prescott waived his right to a demo. He could see from the various restraining devices and the variety of wires, chains, needles, and electrodes assembled that any sort of demonstration would scar him for life. He loaded it into the ship's cargo bay and tied it down to stop it from crashing about during flight. He set the coordinates for surge and placed the ship on autopilot while he went online to arrange a date with a thirty-year-old housewife from the Southern Quarter who was wont to meet him at the border between North and South for a night of simulated lewdness in a rundown motel.

He was just in the process of organizing a time to meet the housewife—from the look of her profile, a digitally enhanced sexpot—when the aft viewfinder began to bleep. He checked the auto scope for signs of activity, but, when there was nothing on the scope that he could immediately identify, he switched to manual and slowly maneuvered the viewfinder a few degrees until he was sure there was nothing behind him. Then he saw it, a five-star Corps raider, stealth class, materializing off his port side.

'What the . . .?'

The ship had a lock on him and fired a warning shot across his bow. Prescott fired up the thrusters and began evasive maneuvers in the hope he could dodge it. The fighter stayed with him. By the time it got another lock, Prescott had raised his shields. The second shot clipped his left wing. The Leadbelly began to spin lazily from the blast impact. Prescott decided to surge early. He would fire the boosters and hopefully hit surge capacity before another of those shots reduced him to space rubble.

Question 1:

What is a corporation raider doing this far north without support?

Question 2:

Why is it attacking us for no apparent reason?

Question 3:

What does it matter when it clearly means to annihilate us?

Question 4:

How the fuck do we outrun it in an interstellar bathtub?

The Leadbelly hit surge capacity. Prescott locked the coordinates in. The fighter locked onto him again. He missed being pulverized by a second at the most. The Leadbelly surged. For a moment there was weightlessness on the ships main deck. Then they were gone. The fighter was off the radar. Prescott took this opportunity to arm the ships floaters, which were deep space blast-boxes with a shock radius of a mile. When released, they would expand and detonate after a five second interval. They would knock out anything that was unlucky enough to get in their way. Stalker and Pymchuck had arrived at the main deck and had seated themselves either side of him.

'It would seem we're discovered, Mr. Pymchuck,' said Stalker.

'Just so, Mr. Stalker,' said Pymchuck.

'What?' said Prescott, nonplussed. 'So you know who that is?'

'We do, Mr. Prescott.'

'Stop calling me Mr. Prescott.'

'Would you prefer Mr. O'Hara?'

The aft viewfinder was bleeping again and there was the raider, appearing out of surge. How in the name of God had it tracked them here? Standard Corps fighters didn't have tracking technology. There was something different about this ship. Another shot deflected off the Leadbelly's right wing, sending it plummeting downward through the bottomless void. It spiraled as it plummeted, throwing both Stalker and Pymchuck about the flight deck like litter. A few more of those would cut the ship in half. His shields had regenerated during surge but they were back down to 50 percent. This was not looking very promising at the moment.

'So what does he want?'

'What does who want, Mr. Prescott?' That was Stalker again, calm as a cucumber in spite of their predicament.

'The psychopath chasing us?'

'Mistress Glum-Shine, I expect.'

'And who's Glum-Shine when she's at home? Do you know her? Is she a stowaway?'

'In a manner of speaking, she's one of the bodies we're carrying.'

'Hold on a sec, I thought you said they were fishermen on board?'

'We did, Mr. Prescott. However, one of them isn't.'

'And there was me, thinking you were mortuary attendants. So who in the name of Billie Holiday is chasing us?'

'Eddie The Dog.'

'The what?'

'The Dog! A dangerous simulant who works for the Pereira Family! I'm sure you're aware of them. They run all of the not so legal freight out of the Northern Quarter. I daresay you've even worked for them in the past. They call him The Dog because he has developed a set of bizarre character traits as a result of being recycled so many times. The Pereira's do like originality in their killers. Still, we plan for all contingencies.'

'Really?' Prescott cursed and shook his head. By way of reply, Stalker pressed his cane into Prescott's belly. For a moment Prescott was at a loss. What on Earth was he prodding him in the belly with his cane for? Then his body went numb and he slipped out of his chair. He slid onto the decking like a coil of old rope. Stalker consulted his fob watch before snapping the case shut. He placed his undertaker's hands on his knees.

'In case you didn't hear me properly,' he intoned, standing up and placing the tip of the cane onto Prescott's thigh. 'We plan for all contingencies. We expected this could happen. If you had stuck to the schedule we would not have been in this fix.' Stalker leaned over Prescott's innate form and shook his skeletal head left to right. 'While you were dallying on Blackstroke with that deviant Marley and his bordello of top-class fetish-whores, I contacted an old friend in the vicinity and organized to be extracted from this wretched hovel at prearranged coordinates. My accomplice, Pymchuck, is at this very moment inputting them into your surge-drive. My apologies, but I daresay you would not have agreed with our plan of action. I shall of course not be paying you for the whole of the voyage since it seems we will no longer be requiring your services. However, I will be leaving you in the company of the Glum-Shine lady, since I took the time on Blackstroke to extract enough of a DNA sample from her to fulfill the obligations of my contract. I shall also leave my brandy on board since the quality of beverages here is lacking. As a token of my good faith, I have not stunned you too badly. I feel I should give you a sporting chance of escaping The Dog even though your service has been minimal at best. And with that I bid you a fond adieu, Mr. Prescott. I daresay given the circumstances, I may not be meeting you again in the future.'

Prescott lay on the deck of the Leadbelly cursing his stupidity. Grave robbers. They were interstellar grave robbers. They were on Evergreen to steal corpses to sell them to the highest bidder! He should have figured it out. He should have known something was wrong. Fishermen freezing to death! Why did he have to be so gullible? There were all manner of deviants out there, especially in the Northern Quarter. Some rich wanker, with a taste for high priced weirdness and illegality, had probably commissioned Stalker and Pymchuck to steal Mistress Glum-Shine. They would have a clone made up of her then sell the clone to whoever had requested it. Celebrity cloning was common. Illegal cloning laboratories were rife across the galaxy.

The ship surged suddenly and Prescott's limp form was tossed about like spaghetti. Then the ship was still. Pymchuck hovered over him briefly. He doffed his hat and smiled like a simpleton. His heavy gut bulged his wrinkled shirt out along the waistline.

'Good luck, Mr. Prescott.' He said and a look of genuine sympathy passed over his moon-face. Then he placed his hands by his side, straightened his back like he was awaiting a military inspection, and was promptly teleported off the bridge. Whoever was picking them up obviously had decent teleport technology. In his place was nothing but the burnt air smell of a recently completed molecular transmission. Stalker was no doubt gone now too. He would have taken his belongings with him, carry-on luggage for the most part, and left the corpses behind. It would possibly be some time before the feeling returned to Prescott's extremities. He could only hope at this point that Eddie the Dog didn't manage to get on board the Leadbelly before he was able to surge out of the area.

A couple of minutes passed. He got the feeling back in his fingertips. He was able to move his hands and feet. He stumbled upright and lurched to the console. About to put a block on incoming teleports, he was too late. The console indicated a breach and someone else on board the ship. It could only be The Dog. He tried to focus. What would Grandmaster Flash do? He heard the distinctive sound of a dog barking, realizing the situation was critical. He shut the doors to the bridge, locking himself in. This was no time for heroics, he reasoned. He localized the heat body signature on the electro map of the ships interior. Eddie the Dog was on the jump deck. Good. He'd flush him out of the airlock. He checked the ship's computer and tapped in the command to flush the airlock. The system was offline. Prescott punched the console. The console warned him to behave himself. Then suddenly, the heat signature disappeared. Prescott's eyes widened. How was that possible? A sudden waft of warm dog smell perforated his nostrils. Prescott started to panic. Eddie the Dog was on the main deck. He'd teleported manually from the jump deck. The jig was up! Shit! Now what was he going to do? Here was a six-foot monster with sharpened teeth and luminous dreadlocks and a canon slung over his shoulder wearing armor plate and a digital dog collar around his neck, staring at him, licking his lips, his black eyes shiny with malicious intent.

Prescott looked for a weapon. His pistol was under his cot pillow. The only potential weapon available was the coffee maker in the corner. He wouldn't get to it in time. He doubted scalding coffee would slow The Dog down by even a nanosecond. There was no time for further consideration. The Dog bounded across the deck, pounced, spun in mid-air and hit him square in the chest with both feet. Prescott was launched through the air. He hit a beam and spun off into the console. He was unconscious less than a minute. When he came to, he was appalled to observe The Dog tossing a severed finger from palm to palm. His mouth dribbled blood. He was grinning like a devil. Prescott's left hand throbbed. The little finger was missing. It was bitten off down to the knuckle. He passed out again. When he came to, The Dog had the canon pointed at him. A shot from that and his head would disintegrate. Prescott ignored the pain in his finger. He attempted to sit upright to reason with his tormentor.

'Now hold on a sec,' he managed before The Dog hit him again. He slashed him with a razor sharp digitally enhanced claw. Warm blood began to soak his hair.

'Where is she?' The Dog growled.

'Cold storage downstairs.'

'And where is Mr. Stalker?'

'I couldn't really say.'

'Grrrr.'

The Dog pulled a blade from his belt. He began to toss it from palm to palm.

'Where's my finger?' Prescott enquired.

'Worry about your throat,' snarled The Dog.

The thing that stopped him crying like a little girl, the thing that stopped him from completely losing it and breaking down, was the pain. It had sharpened his focus. He'd feel sorry for himself later. He was grateful nothing was broken. He'd hit that cross beam with some force. He was lucky his back hadn't been snapped. Also, it was his left hand that had the finger missing. He was right handed. Talk about the upside of down. The Dog was on him again. He was inches from his face. He thought he would bite his nose off. His hot breath smelled meaty. Prescott felt like retching. The Dog's black eyes bored holes in his skull.

'This will hurt,' he said, 'but I need your full attention.'

The Dog slammed the blade into Prescott's shoulder and Prescott shot upright through the shock of the pain.

'Now,' said the Dog, 'where do we begin?' He flicked the back of his ear. It was like he had fleas to contend with. Does he lick his own balls too? Prescott wondered. However, the contemplation was short-lived.

'There shall be no negotiations until the body is located. After that, you will have ten minutes to convince me not to kill you. If you convince me not to kill you, you will have a ten-minute head start. Then I will give chase. I will hunt you. I will disable your ship and tow you to the nearest derelict moon. Then I will board your ship again. At this point I suggest suicide. I'm sure if they could, my previous victims would recommend not being eaten.'

Prescott felt his bowels loosen at the thought of acting as an impartial witness to his own intestines being chewed.

I'll tell him where Stalker's headed, he reasoned, then I'll give him the money Stalker paid me. Then I'll offer him the brandy. If all else fails, I'll give him the restraint device. Maybe that will cheer him up a bit.

The Dog hunkered onto his haunches. 'Your ten minutes starts now . . .'

Prescott offered up the destination of Stalker and Pymchuck. That wasn't good enough. He told him about the DNA sample they'd extracted. That wasn't good enough either. He offered the money and that wasn't good enough. Finally, he offered him the brandy thinking how sad it was the only thing he had to bargain with was alcohol. Surprisingly, The Dog seemed happy with this. He snatched the blade out of Prescott's shoulder. He growled showing those terrible pointed teeth. Then he located the body on the console and transported it to the raider. Slinging the canon over his shoulder, he dropped down onto all fours, urinating onto the decking before bounding off toward the jump deck, where he would teleport back to his raider.

'Your ten minutes just started over . . .' he barked, and then he was gone.

Prescott hoped that he was sick on his arrival back at the raider. Jumping through space like that always made folk sick. Simulants were different though. It might not impact on him the same as it did humans.

Prescott clambered onto his seat. He faced the console. Loss of blood and pain made his head swim. He couldn't outrun The Dog, not if it could track him when he surged. He wondered where the tracking device was located. It must have come aboard with Glum-Shine's corpse. That meant that it had to have left with her as well. Still, The Dog was clever. He would have attached another. There was no time to locate it though. He only had ten minutes to jump away. He considered doubling back on himself. The Dog would track him if he did that. He considered hiding out somewhere. Again The Dog would track him. Then an idea occurred to him, which was risky to say the least, but it was better than nothing, which was his only alternative. Sure, the chances of survival were limited. Still, the thought of having his liver removed and stir fried in a wok while he looked on in terror was a worse proposition. Also, there were no other options left to him. He could drop a blast-box, but knowing the raider, it would simply dodge the floaters then blast them into nothing. So what was left? What could he do to dodge the inevitable? The closest planet according to his star charts was the planet Halibut where the negotiations were taking place. Once there he could make a lot of noise and hope that when Eddie arrived he surged into a shit rain. Prescott typed the coordinates in for Halibut. He punched the console and the Leadbelly surged.

In his haste to get to Halibut, he came out of the surge late, crashed into the negotiations vessel and all hell broke loose. The vessel was parked off the fishing planet. Two destroyers were stationed nearby. They were there to make sure negotiations ran smoothly. One represented the Southern Corporations. The other represented the Northern Federation. They were supposed to be in attendance for show as a deterrent. Nobody was really expecting any trouble to break out. There were demonstrations planned to take place but they were expected on Halibut, not in its orbit.

Thus when the Leadbelly appeared, it was something of a shock. Prescott tried to dodge the vessel. He was going too fast. The vessel was too big. Collision was inevitable. He braced himself for impact. However, its defenses were up. The Leadbelly's were also up, since it had recently been the victim of an attack from the raider. This meant that both ships bounced off one another harmlessly like rubber.

The Dog, meanwhile, hot on the Leadbelly's trail appeared soon after. The Northern Federation targeted. They assumed it was a corps raider. Nobody thought it stupid that the South would send a solitary ship, no matter how souped-up it appeared, to wreak havoc on proceedings.

The negotiations had started already. The diplomats and trade representatives wouldn't be able to evacuate in time. Nevertheless, those officers commanding the northern destroyer assumed foul play. The Dog got a missile lock on the Leadbelly, which was out of control and spinning lazily toward the northern destroyer. A general panic ensued. The raider's missiles, which were meant to cripple the Leadbelly and render it helpless, latched onto the heat signature of the northern destroyer instead. Just at that moment, the northern destroyer was in the process of aiming it's not insubstantial weaponry at everybody all at once, unsure of who was the enemy and who firstly they should open fire on.

The upshot of this was that The Dog's missiles disabled the northern destroyer's weapons momentarily thus providing the Leadbelly with the perfect escape route. Prescott took advantage of this and bashed in coordinates. The Leadbelly surged, almost instantly to safety. The southern corporation's destroyer opened fire on both the raider and the northern destroyer. The northern destroyer was slow in getting its shields up. It sustained heavy losses before eventually regrouping. Power was ultimately restored. It was able to contact its opposite number to negotiate a cease-fire.

The Leadbelly was forgotten temporarily. The Dog surged to an unknown destination, to try to reorganize and to lick his wounds. Prescott, meanwhile, following the surge, set about locating the tracking device The Dog had embedded. The Dog had planted four of the little blighters on the ship. They were free-roamers too, which meant they scurried about the ship on digitally modified legs. Once that was sorted he ejected the dead fishermen, along with the free roamers out of the airlock, then he headed back to Evergreen to hand over his cargo.

He had a new finger attached. It was biomechanical, recycled, and inexpensive. He'd briefly contemplated revenge, but then decided it was too much bother. If he ever bumped into the grave robbers again, he would be sure to torture them with a blowtorch, douse them in combustible fluids, and set fire to them both before dumping them in an asteroid belt. For now, however, he was done with the pair of them. The Dog and The Pereira Family would be on the lookout for him, a not inconsiderable enemy with plenty of resources to draw upon. He would have to keep his head down for a while. He would lay low, wait for the dust to settle, chill out, read a book.

Thus, having parked the Leadbelly on the planet Evergreen, close to the Northern Ledge in an attempt to remain inconspicuous, Prescott O'Hara hoisted his feet onto the console. He lit up a joint that he'd constructed from some of the leftover juju weed. He closed his eyes . . .

. . .and considered the future.

ABOUT THE AUTHOR

Mark Anthony Ayling

Mark Anthony Ayling is a 38-year-old registered mental health nurse living in the northwest of England in the city of Salford. He was born and raised in St Helens where he spent his formative years reading horror, fantasy, science fiction stories, and comics and listening to as much decent music as he could possibly get his hands on. He eventually went to university to study English Literature and French and later decided to complete a diploma in nursing.

Mark helps to run an introduction to creative writing course for the recovery academy at the mental health trust where he works, as a community psychiatric nurse. He attends a speculative writers group called Manchester

Speculative Writer's Group in Manchester, which is a lot of fun for him.

Mark is happily married (most of the time) and has a 4-year-old son named Sam and 2-year-old daughter named Molly. He spends whatever spare time he can salvage writing stories (often late at night), rearranging his record collection, going to watch live music, attending rugby league games, and watching films. *Northern Futures* is his first collection of short stories.

In addition to stories in this collection that were previously published by *Perihelion Online Science Fiction Magazine*, Mark had a story published in the now defunct (unfortunately) *Cracked Eye Online Magazine*, and "Prodigious" appeared in *Twisted Tails IX: Wunderkind*, edited by J. Richard Jacobs.

Books from Lillicat Publishers

Visions Series
Visions: Leaving Earth (2014)
Visions II: Moons of Saturn (2015)
Visions III: Inside the Kuiper Belt (2015)
Visions IV: Space Between Stars (May 2016)
Visions V: Milky Way (August 2016)
Visions VI: Galaxies (November 2016)

TreeVolution (November 2016)
Northern Futures (December 2016)
The Future Is Short: Science Fiction in a Flash (2014)
Sunshine & Shadow: Memories from a Long Life (2014)

VISIONS VI: *GALAXIES*

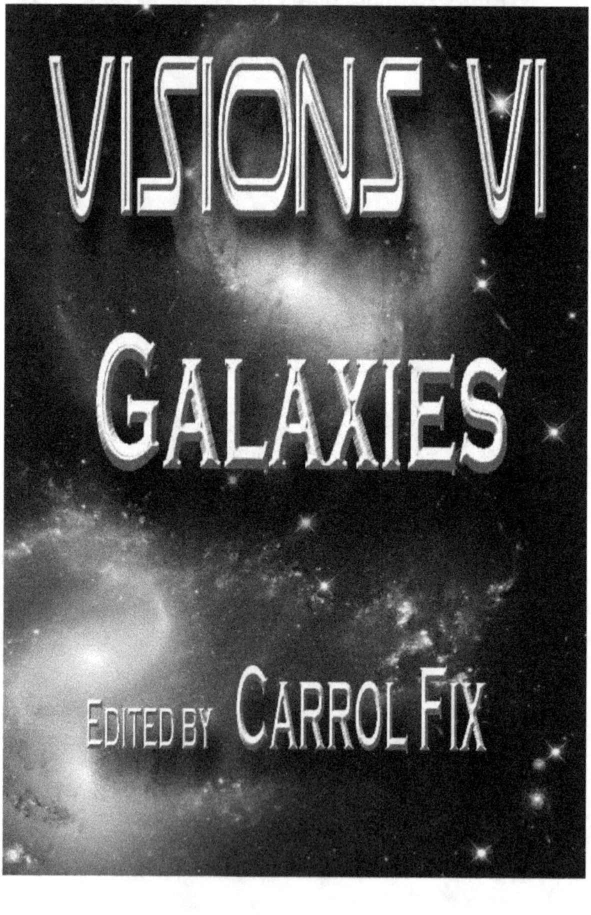

VISIONS IV: SPACE BETWEEN STARS

VISIONS III: *INSIDE THE KUIPER BELT*

VISIONS II: MOONS OF SATURN

VISIONS: LEAVING EARTH

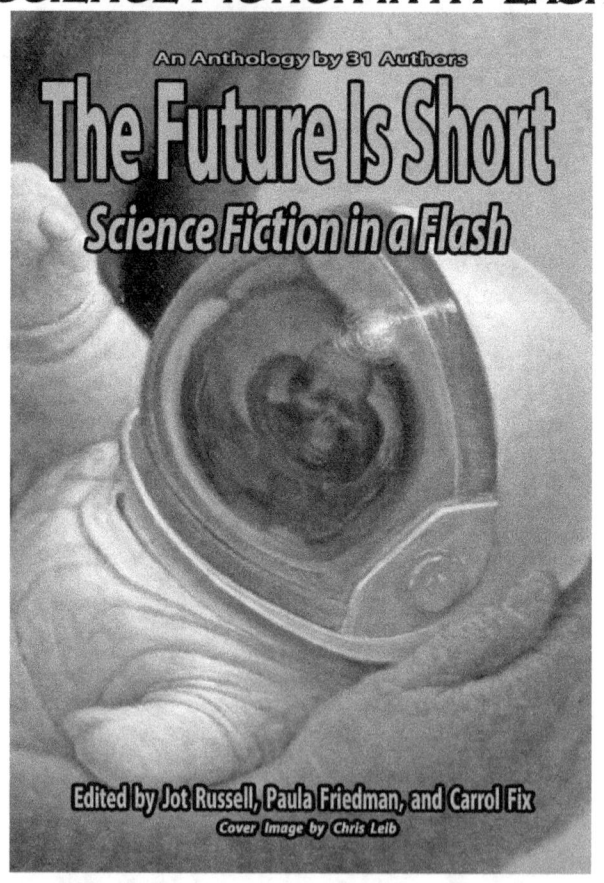

. . . and coming soon!

VISIONS VII: UNIVERSE